Other Books by Evelyn Sibley Lampman

White Captives

Rattlesnake Cave

Go Up the Road

The Potlatch Family

(MARGARET K. MC ELDERRY BOOKS)

Bargain Bride

EVELYN SIBLEY LAMPMAN

Bargain Bride

A MARGARET K. MC ELDERRY BOOK

ATHENEUM · 1977 · NEW YORK

Library of Congress Cataloging in Publication Data

Lampman, Evelyn Sibley.   Bargain bride.
"A Margaret K. McElderry book."
Summary: Because married settlers could claim
twice the land of a bachelor, orphaned Ginny was
married when she was ten-years-old. Now fifteen,
her husband comes to claim her.
[1.   Oregon—History—To 1859—Fiction.
2.   Orphans—Fiction]   I.   Title.
PZ7.L185Bar   [Fic]   76-46567
ISBN 0-689-50075-0

Published simultaneously in Canada by
McClelland & Stewart, Ltd.
Manufactured in the United States of America
by American Book-Stratford Press, Inc.
Designed by Suzanne Haldane
First Printing March 1977
Second Printing August 1977

Bargain Bride

chapter one

*I*t was still dark when Ginny woke up, but she knew it was morning. Something in her bones told her so. For a few moments she lay doubled into a ball under the thin quilts, then it all came back to her. She began to shiver as though she had an attack of the ague, and the shaking wouldn't stop. It had finally come, the day she had been dreading for the past five years. This was her birthday. Today she was fifteen years old.

Before long she heard Cousin Mattie stirring around in the cabin, ordering Cousin Beau to get out of bed and poke up the fire. Cousin Mattie never talked in ordinary tones like other folks. Her voice was loud, with a nasal twang, and she was generally giving orders. People better jump when she opened her mouth, too.

Ginny could hear her voice as plain as anything because there was only a thin calico curtain shutting off the corner of the room where she slept. There wouldn't have been that except for Julia Bridges.

Two years before when the Bridges had sent Julia to board with Mattie and Beau Danville so she could attend Mr. Lyle's school, Cousin Mattie had hung up the strip of cloth. She said Mrs. Bridges gave herself airs and probably wouldn't pay the two dollars a month board if Julia had to sleep in the same room with Cousin Beau and Cousin Mattie. It was all right for her to share Ginny's bed, though. They were both girls. No one had suggested that Ginny attend school. Schools cost money.

Now Julia must be boarding with somebody else because Mr. Lyle had moved his school to the larger town of Dallas two miles away, the seat of Polk County in the Oregon territory.

Ginny missed Julia, and she was thankful that the curtain was still there. Cousin Mattie kept saying she was going to take it down and make the cloth into something useful. She hadn't got around to it yet.

A spot of yellow, like a baby moon, shone through the printed calico and Ginny knew that Cousin Mattie had lighted one of her grease candles. There was a thumping sound as Cousin Beau turned over the oak log that had been smoldering all night in the fireplace, and more bumps as he threw on dry fir that would catch quickly.

"Ginny!" shouted Cousin Mattie. "Get out of bed!

4

Orville, Willie! Stir yourselves out of that loft and get down here. We got a busy day ahead of us."

Orville and Willie always had to be called twice, but Ginny never stayed in bed after she was called. She was too scared of Cousin Mattie. Not that Cousin Mattie did any more than switch her legs with a hazel bush stick or send her to bed without supper. But she *could* do more if she wanted. She was the meanest woman Ginny knew. At least, this is the last time she can scream at me to get up, she told herself. Whatever was going to happen couldn't be much worse than living with Cousin Mattie.

She put on her old patched dress that was too short in the sleeves and so tight across the chest that it gaped between the buttons. Her good one, the one she would wear when she left, had been washed and starched and was hanging from a nail in the wall. It was a little tight, too, but Ginny would never give it up because it had been cut down for her from one of her mother's dresses. It was muslin, and once there had been yellow rosebuds on it, though they had faded so you could hardly see them. She could remember when Mama wore it and how pretty she had looked. Ginny didn't think she herself would ever be that pretty. She looked more like Papa with her dark red hair and brown eyes and freckles. People used to say she had Papa's spunk, too, but Cousin Mattie had knocked that out of her. Cousin Mattie said spunk wasn't fitting in a young girl, and maybe she was right. Mama had been sweet and gentle, and people were always trying to do things for her. Nobody tried to do anything for Ginny. They hadn't since she was ten.

"There you are," said Cousin Mattie, when she

5

pushed back the curtain. "Go wash up. Then hurry with the milking. We don't know when Mr. Mayhew will get here, and I shouldn't care to have him catch us all at sixes and sevens."

"I don't figure he'll make it before noon, Mattie." Cousin Beau turned his backside to the fire to warm himself. "Told me he had to collect his wheat at Jim Driscoll's mill, then drive it in to Dallas. It'll be noon at the earliest. Maybe later."

"And what are we supposed to do, I should like to know?" snapped Cousin Mattie. "In common decency we got to give the man dinner when he gets here. Do we have to wait around till maybe one or two o'clock to eat ourselves?"

Ginny didn't wait to hear what Cousin Beau said. She knew it would be something to smooth Cousin Mattie's feathers. Cousin Beau spent his life smoothing Cousin Mattie's ruffled feathers.

As she let the bucket down into the well and hauled it up, she wondered again why Cousin Beau had ever married his wife in the first place. Mama and Papa had wondered about it too. Once, when they didn't know she was listening, she had heard them talking about it.

Cousin Beau was Mama's second cousin once removed. His branch of the family had moved to Georgia years before, so the Danvilles who stayed in North Carolina seldom saw them. "Still, they're kissing cousins," Mama had insisted. "We're bound to be civil to them."

Cousin Beau had been sent up north to school, which Papa said was silly since the south had perfectly good schools of its own. Mama agreed and said probably the family was sorry in the end because while he was there he married Cousin Mattie. He brought her home, but she didn't get along too well with people, so she and Cousin Beau moved away, to Illinois or somewhere.

The first time Mama or Papa ever laid eyes on them was when they appeared in the same wagon train headed west. Cousin Beau's wagon wasn't nearly as good as Papa's, and he didn't have extra stock like most folks, but when Mama heard the name "Danville," which was the same as hers before she was married, she had to speak up. Cousin Beau and Cousin Mattie were glad to meet their cousins, but Papa said Mama should have kept her pretty mouth closed.

The well water was icy cold when Ginny washed her hands and face, and the towel that hung on a peg was clammy and didn't do a good job drying. In a way she didn't blame Orville and Willie, who usually didn't wash with water but just swiped a damp towel across their faces.

Orville and Willie were horrible little boys. Ginny thought about them as little as possible, but Cousin Mattie doted on them both. Maybe that was because they looked more like her than their father and every day they acted more like her, too. They were ten and eleven now, but five years ago, when they first came here, Ginny's chief responsibility had been looking after them. They were always doing something they shouldn't, then Ginny was blamed for letting them do it. Afterwards they'd smirk behind their mother's back and wiggle their fingers in their ears at Ginny as though to say, "Look what we did!" She hated Orville and Willie almost as much as she did Cousin Mattie, and the one good thing about today was that it might be the last time she'd ever have to see them.

It was getting light now. The sky was pink above the stand of firs that Cousin Beau had been meaning to log off for the past five years. There was frost glistening under her old, cracked shoes, and she pulled the gray knitted shawl more closely round her. It was cold that morning. People said it was always balmy in Oregon, but they were wrong.

It was warmer in the barn though. The neighbors had given the Danvilles a barn-raising, and the men had caulked the logs up good and tight. If Cousin Beau had done it by himself, it wouldn't have been so good a job. Cousin Beau tried. He jumped when Cousin Mattie told him to, but he always petered out before the end of anything.

Dolly was standing in her stall, waiting to be milked. By rights the cow should have been Ginny's. Dolly's mother had been Star, the milk cow Papa brought from North Carolina.

When both her parents came down with the cholera on the Platte and were dead in twenty-four hours, Cousin Beau had taken over Star along with Papa's wagon and everything he owned. He said it was only fitting since he was kinfolks and meant to do for the pitiful little orphan, Ginny, like she was his own. Cousin Mattie drove their wagon and Cousin Beau drove Papa's, but pretty soon the Danville wagon fell apart and wasn't worth fixing. They all crowded into Papa's. There was nothing but trouble afterwards. Indians ran off with most of the stock, and little by little they had to discard things by the way. Ginny didn't know how Star managed to survive, but she had.

And now here was her daughter, waiting to be milked. Ginny felt she owed Dolly an explanation.

"I have to go away, Dolly," she said. "I won't see you ever again. But I'll think about you sometimes, and I hope it's Cousin Beau or maybe Willie who comes to milk you. I think they'd be the nicest to you."

Dolly turned and regarded her with soft brown eyes. It was almost as though she understood and was sorry. For the first time, Ginny put her head against the warm flank and began to cry. How awful to think that the only one in the whole world who cared what happened to her was a cow!

She hadn't cried since they left the Platte where she had watched Mama and Papa, wrapped in blankets, being lowered into the hastily dug graves. Then wagons had been run over the mounds to flatten them. People said it was so wild animals or Indians wouldn't dig up the bodies. It didn't seem right to leave them there, but there was nothing Ginny could do about it.

The day after the burial she stopped crying, but it was like she was living outside her own body and the things that happened to her were happening to someone else.

When she looked back, she could hardly remember the rest of the trip. Memories of it came only in snatches, like random pages in a book. Over and over the snatches were of Cousin Beau and Cousin Mattie pestering her about what Papa had done with his money. Ginny didn't know, but they kept after her until they reached Oregon.

She seemed to recall walking a great distance beside the wagon and of long waits while the wagons were lowered over cliffs on ropes. She thought there was a cold, wet ride down a swirling river that lasted several days, but she didn't remember much about it. She could dimly remember stopping at a fort enclosed by a stockade, and a tall gentleman with white hair and a flowing black cape who patted her on the head and called her a pretty little girl. He was nice, and she wished she could have stayed there instead of going on with Cousin Beau and Cousin Mattie.

She remembered arriving in Oregon City and how cross Cousin Mattie was. There was free land all right, but it was winter and who could live on uncleared land with no cabin and no food? And the boarding house where they were staying wanted to be paid, and there was no money. What did Cousin Beau propose to do about that?

Then there was the last page out of the book. They had gone to someone's house, Ginny in her least ragged dress and worn-out shoes, Cousin Beau and Cousin Mattie and their sons, Orville and Willie. There were two strange men there, and one was a preacher. Ginny could tell by his collar. The other was a tall, broad-shouldered man with a red face. He took Ginny's hand and they stood in front of the preacher, who said some words. They concluded with, "Now I pronounce you man and wife."

When the preacher was through speaking, the stranger, who was holding her hand, turned to her.

10

"They explained this to you, didn't they, little lady? We may be married, but you're still going to live with your folks till you're fifteen. There won't be no difference at all. It's just because of the land. A married man can file a claim on six hundred and forty acres, but a single one, he only gets three hundred and twenty. Come fifteen, you'll find I've made things nice and proper for you. You'll have as good a house as I can build, maybe even planed lumber, not a cabin made of logs. I'll treat you right, little lady. You don't need to be scared."

That's how Miss Virginia Claibourn, ten years old, became Mrs. Virginia Mayhew. It was scary to think of.

Once she had told Julia Bridges about it, but Julia didn't seem to think it was so bad as Ginny did.

"It happens all the time in Oregon," she had said. "You're not the only one. You don't have to live with your husband till you're fifteen. That's a proper age. It's when I intend to get married. I wouldn't want people to start calling me an old maid, and they would if I waited too long. You'll never have to worry about that. I'm going to pick my own husband, though. Mama said I could, so long as I pick somebody that's comfortably fixed."

Somehow Julia's words had done little to comfort Ginny. She'd rather risk being called an old maid.

Right after the wedding, the Danville family moved from the boarding house in Oregon City to land in the lush Willamette Valley. There was even a cabin on it and several cleared acres. A squatter had lived there without bothering to file his claim, and Cousin Beau had bought him out. There were settled claims close by, each a mile square, and Cousin Beau was delighted to find that their owners were largely southerners like himself. Cousin Mattie wasn't so pleased and made scathing remarks about Colonel Ford, who had brought three Negroes along to do the field and housework. Southerners were all lazy, she insisted. Give her a good, hard-working Yankee any day. She'd got out of the South once, and now here she was surrounded by so many people from Virginia, Kentucky, Tennessee, and the Carolinas that folks called the area Little Dixie. Still it was land, free land, and she guessed beggars couldn't be choosers.

After they moved in, Ginny's life was no longer composed of brief, unconnected events, but took on a daily monotony of work. She had never done physical labor before, but she did now. Cousin Mattie taught her. There were dishes to do and scrubbing, washing and ironing, candles to make, cooking in pots hung on the crane above the fireplace, the cow to milk and the milk to be cared for, the cream made into butter, and what was left turned into cottage cheese or slopped to the pig. It was work, work, work from can't-see to can't-see, and then fall into bed so tired she could hardly put one foot ahead of the other. If she let up for a minute, Cousin Mattie would yell at her, just as she would yell now if Ginny didn't stop crying and get on with her job.

She wiped her eyes on the gray shawl and resumed the milking, but her mind was still busy. Today Mr. Mayhew was coming to claim his bride. What would her life be like on his claim near the headwaters of the La Creole? Would it be harder than the one she knew now? Would she wish she were back, listening to Cousin Mattie yell and Cousin Beau make promises he wouldn't keep and the boys' teasing? If only Papa and Mama and Ginny hadn't left North Carolina in the first place! If only they'd never met Cousin Beau on that wagon train and he hadn't bought out the squatter's claim!

Her hands slowed almost as soon as the milk began spurting regularly into the bucket. For the first time a horrifying thought came to her. Where had Cousin Beau got the money to pay the squatter for his claim? He had none when he arrived, only enough borrowed from the Hudson's Bay Company to pay for seed. Most of the settlers had borrowed from the English company for their first crops, and while Cousin Beau had taken longer than most to repay his debt, Ginny knew he had done so. Cousin Mattie, who refused to be beholden to anyone had seen to that. She didn't want the neighbors to talk. There was only one person who could have given Cousin Beau the money, and that person was Mr. Mayhew. It was in exchange for three hundred and twenty acres of land, a wife's share, of a donation land claim. How stupid she had been not to think of it before!

"You 'bout done, Ginny honey?" asked a voice from the doorway. "Your Cousin Mattie sent me to fetch you. She says the milking's taking a mighty long time this morning, and breakfast's ready."

"You sold me!" Ginny turned so abruptly that she almost upset the pail. "You sold me to Mr. Mayhew."

Cousin Beau didn't deny it, and his face above the flowing black beard flushed red.

"Now, honey, you got to think about that a little. Stephen Mayhew's a real fine gentleman. He's got a nice claim, and folks tell he's built a real house, not just a cabin like ours. One of the first houses in Oregon Territory, so you can see he's got your interest at heart. Folks say he came back from California last year with a sizable poke of gold dust, too, so you won't want for anything."

"But he paid you, didn't he? To let him marry me? That old man!"

"He's not so old. Forty maybe. No older. And he don't look that," argued Cousin Beau. His voice took on an apologetic whine. "You got to look at it this way, honey. There wasn't nothing else to do but borrow from Stephen Mayhew. I aim to pay him back, and I will. Rest assured of that."

"You didn't even ask me," she said. "You just married me off."

"You were too young to know your own mind. And besides, you're not the only young girl here that was married that way. There's a lot of them. Been happening since folks learned about that law giving a wife her own three hundred and twenty acres. I did what was best for you. I arranged a good marriage. Why, it happens to kings and queens all the time. Sometimes I wonder if marriages like that don't turn out better. Oft times young people get carried away, but you can't tell them nothing," Cousin Beau concluded thoughtfully.

There was no use arguing with him, Ginny thought. She resumed the milking, her fingers closing and opening so fiercely that Dolly turned in surprise.

"You hurry along now, hear?" Cousin Beau said cheerfully. "Like I say, breakfast's on the table."

They were almost finished eating when Ginny arrived at the cabin.

"What took you so long?" demanded Cousin Mattie. "We got no time to dawdle today. Your mush is cold, but you'll have to eat it that way. I already dished up."

"She's all agog. Her husband's coming to fetch her. Ain't he, Mrs. Mayhew?" said Orville, snickering.

"No. She's been crying. Likely she's skeered he'll beat her." Willie's little black eyes were on her swollen face. For just a moment he sounded sympathetic. Then he glanced at his brother and began to giggle.

"Quiet, both of you," ordered Cousin Beau sternly. It was so unusual that his sons stared at him in amazement. Generally their mother was the one who took care of corrections in the family.

Cousin Mattie seemed surprised, too. She looked at Cousin Beau curiously before she tilted her bowl to get the last few drops of sugar-sweetened milk.

Ginny sat down at her place and measured out a spoonful of brown sugar for her mush before flooding it with milk. She wondered if Mr. Mayhew would be as strict about the use of sugar as Cousin Mattie. If he had all that money, he might let her have as much as she wanted.

"We'll bake up a couple of squash pies," said Cousin Mattie, changing the subject. "Mr. Mayhew might have a fancy for them. Living alone that way, he wouldn't get pie every day. And we'll put a piece of that pork on the spit. You can't overcook pork, and we don't know what time he'll get here."

"You fixing a banquet, Ma?" asked Orville, grinning.

"Hush your mouth," ordered Cousin Mattie. "It's just a family dinner. Mr. Mayhew is family now, and when we go to visit, I reckon he'll do it up proud for us."

15

You'll never come to visit if I can do anything about it, thought Ginny silently. When I leave here, I never want to see any of you again. Ever.

As usual Cousin Mattie kept her running from one task to another all morning. Not that Cousin Mattie didn't work, too. Ginny had to say that much for her. Cousin Mattie seldom sat down, and when she did, her hands were busy with mending clothes or knitting shawls or endless stockings for her family.

Today she insisted on cleaning the cabin thoroughly, taking the straw ticks, which served as mattresses, outside and shaking them, scrubbing the board floor, which was about the only improvement Cousin Beau had got around to making in the squatter's cabin, peeling squash, and mixing dough that would bake in the Dutch oven into crusty, mouth-watering pies, turning the slab of pork that hung over the fire, and setting the table with odds and ends of crockery.

Once, in the midst of all their bustle, she said an amazing thing. She looked up from where she was scrubbing the floor on her hands and knees and remarked, "Mr. Mayhew will find you're a real good worker, Ginny. Reckon maybe I'll notice it around here when you're gone."

Ginny was so surprised she could only stare open-mouthed, and Cousin Mattie frowned and told her to stop gaping and get back to work.

She was so busy that it was almost a surprise when Willie pushed open the door and announced, "He's here. Mr. Mayhew's come for Ginny."

"Quick!" Cousin Mattie ordered. "Leave things. I'll

finish. We're almost done anyhow. Go change to your good dress. Mr. Mayhew can't see you looking like that. Comb your hair, too."

Ginny dropped the handle of the spit she had been turning and straightened up. The moment had come. It was actually here, and there was nothing she could do to prolong it. She turned and fled behind the calico curtain to the little cubbyhole that held her bed.

chapter two

*T*his here's for you, Miss—er—Ginny," said Mr. Mayhew awkwardly. His perpetually red face flushed even darker as he held out the newspaper-wrapped parcel.

Ginny, who had not spoken since she emerged from her curtained corner, looked at him in astonishment. It was the first time she had been able to glance in his direction, and suddenly she realized that Stephen Mayhew was as embarrassed as she was.

"A present!" cried Cousin Mattie.

"Now ain't that thoughtful?" approved Cousin Beau. "Go take it, honey. And save the paper. Not often we get a look at a newspaper around here."

"A piece of the *Oregon Spectator*." Stephen Mayhew turned to him eagerly as though he might be glad to look away from Ginny. "Not over two weeks old, neither. The lady in Dallas, she wrapped it up for me when I told her it was a present."

Ginny took two hesitant steps across the room, and her fingers closed over the parcel. It was limp and yielding in her grasp.

"Go on," ordered Cousin Mattie impatiently. "Open it."

As the paper fell away in her hands, Ginny's fingers felt a softness that she had known only in childhood. Velvet! A moment later she was staring at a bonnet with a curling feather that draped down one side.

"Oh, my stars!" gasped Cousin Mattie. "It must have set you back a pretty penny, Mr. Mayhew."

"What is it?" demanded Orville and Willie in unison.

"A handsome present indeed," said Cousin Beau, reaching for the newspaper wrapping. "I reckon it's been years since I saw a lady wear a bonnet like that. Put it on, Ginny, honey."

Ginny's hands trembled so she could hardly pull the velvet bonnet down on her head, much less tie the matching brown silk strings.

"I recollected Miss Ginny had brown eyes," mumbled Mr. Mayhew. "The bonnet's the same color."

"See that you don't give yourself airs, young lady, just 'cause you got a fine bonnet," Cousin Mattie warned. There was a tinge of envy in her tone.

"Lady in Dallas, she's opened up a millinery store," explained Mr. Mayhew. He seemed pleased that his gift was so well received. "I figured Miss Ginny ought to have something to mark the occasion."

"It's very pretty. Thank you," Ginny told him, trying not to look at Orville who, behind Mr. Mayhew's back, had stuck his fingers in his ears and was wiggling them at her. She wished there were a mirror so she could see how she looked in the new bonnet, but Mama's little hand mirror had disappeared long ago. Probably it had been used in trade for something useful.

"Lay it off now," ordered Cousin Mattie. "Time enough to put it on when you leave. We got dinner to get on the table. Everybody's famished around here."

Ginny carried the bonnet into her corner and placed it gently on the bed. It was nice of Mr. Mayhew to buy her a present. Was he going to be a friend after all?

When they sat down at the table to eat pork and baked sweet potatoes, turnip greens and parsnips, she glanced at him shyly. The stranger sitting there was her husband, she reminded herself. In the five years that had elapsed since that hasty marriage in Oregon City, she had seen him only a few times and then very briefly. Several times he had stopped by the cabin, but he hadn't come in. He had talked with Cousin Beau outside, and Ginny had peeked at him from the window. This was really her first close inspection of the man with whom she was pledged to spend the remainder of her life.

He was a big man, with a sandy beard and bristling eyebrows. He used his knife to eat with more than his fork, but his pale blue eyes were gentle. If only he weren't so old! He caught her staring at him once and smiled briefly before he looked back at his plate.

He's shy, Ginny decided. Willie was wrong. Mr. Mayhew didn't look the kind of man who would beat his wife.

Cousin Mattie did most of the talking, with Cousin Beau throwing in an occasional remark. Most of her conversation was about how hard she had worked to make Ginny into a respectable housewife. Why, she'd had to teach the girl everything, how to wash and clean and cook and even knit. Ginny had been worthless before she came under Cousin Mattie's care. She hadn't known a thing.

As she listened, Ginny felt her face grow warm with resentment. The way Cousin Mattie carried on made it seem that she had been neglected, that her parents had let her grow up ignorant. True, she had never been taught housewifely chores. Back home there had always been someone else to do them. But for three years Ginny had attended Miss Spencer's School for Young Ladies where she had learned to read and write and cipher a little. She had learned to sew tiny seams and embroider samplers, to make a proper curtsy and speak in a soft voice. It wasn't fair to Mama and Papa for Cousin Mattie to talk that way before a stranger.

"I can read." Ginny was as surprised as anyone to hear herself speaking in her own defense. "I can write, too, and do numbers."

"That's not what we're talking about." Cousin Mattie frowned. "What good does book learning do when there's a house to run? Mr. Mayhew don't need that in a wife."

"But it's good to have," insisted Mr. Mayhew. "Book

learning is. I never had none myself. Maybe you could learn me to write my name, Miss Ginny, so I won't have to make a X on the line."

"She'd be pleased to," Cousin Mattie assured him quickly. "I admit there's times when such things come in useful. Beau, here, he's had a lot of book learning. Though there's lots of things he could have learned that would have stood him better through the years."

"I was going to be a lawyer. Maybe even a judge," said Cousin Beau. His voice was a little wistful. "Only I didn't finish."

"Who's ready for pie?" demanded Cousin Mattie quickly. "A nice piece of squash pie'd go down pretty good, wouldn't it, Mr. Mayhew?"

Mr. Mayhew pronounced the pie delicious, but he wouldn't have a second piece.

"We best get started home," he told them. "It's a good seven miles, and the road's bad in spots. Won't make it before dark as it is."

Ginny got to her feet obediently. She looked at the table littered with dirty dishes and took silent pleasure in knowing that Cousin Mattie would have to do them to-day. For the last time she pushed back the calico curtain and then reached for her new bonnet on the bed. It seemed to give her courage, an assurance she thought she had lost.

"You got no satchel?" asked Mr. Mayhew in surprise, when she said she was ready.

"Just this bundle." It contained her other change of underwear and a nightgown. She had left the worn-out dress on the bed for Cousin Mattie to use as rags. The cloth was rotten and wouldn't go through another washing.

"Leastwise get a wrap. It's cold outside," he told her.

"You can take the gray shawl by the door," Cousin Mattie offered generously. "We keep it there, Mr. Mayhew, so whichever of us is about to step outside can slip it on. But I'm knitting a new one, and Ginny's welcome to that."

Ginny started to reach for the shawl, then dropped her hands. The shawl was old and ragged. It was beginning to unravel on one end, and a long strand of yarn trailed to the floor beneath it. Besides, it smelled a little of the barnyard. The old shawl would put the fine new bonnet to shame.

"Thank you, Cousin Mattie," she said primly. "I'll leave it for you. I won't wear anything."

"But you got to have something," insisted Mr. Mayhew. "It's coming on a rain. You'd catch your death."

"Take it, Ginny," ordered Cousin Mattie in her sternest voice. "It's the only wrap you got. Mr. Mayhew's right. You can't go out without something to wrap up in."

"I'll take my mother's shawl," said Ginny. "You've got it shut up in that box under your bed."

"The paisley shawl!" gasped Cousin Mattie. "My paisley? Your ma give it to me herself."

"No, she didn't," said Ginny. If Mr. Mayhew hadn't brought her the bonnet and taken her side in the discussion of book learning, she would never have dared to speak so. But maybe, just maybe, he would back her up.

If he didn't—well, she had nothing to lose. "Mama would never have given away her paisley shawl. She loved it too much. If she gave it away, I'd have known about it."

"You wasn't there," argued Cousin Mattie. "It was that last day, the day she passed on. That's when she give it to me. She meant for me to have it."

"Maybe you misunderstood her, Mattie," said Cousin Beau. His tone was mild, but his voice contained an unexpected note of masculine authority. "And even if you didn't, it would be a nice thing to give Ginny her mama's shawl on the day she's leaving. Ginny's done a lot for us, remember."

"Beau!" gasped Cousin Mattie. Two red spots flamed on her cheeks, and Ginny held her breath wondering what would happen next. Never had she heard Cousin Beau stand up to his wife that way.

To her surprise nothing happened. The indignant fire in Cousin Mattie's eyes dissolved into bewilderment. Her tense shoulders drooped, and without a word she crossed the room and slid the wooden box containing her treasures from under the bed. The paisley shawl was folded on top of everything else. She lifted it out as though it was something she disdained to touch and threw it across the room.

"That's real pretty." Mr. Mayhew stepped forward to catch the shawl before it touched the floor. Now he unfolded it and laid it across Ginny's shoulders. "I ain't surprised your ma set such store by it, Miss Ginny. Not everybody's got a shawl like that out here."

There was mist in the air when they came outside. Cousin Beau had sent the boys to harness Mr. Mayhew's horses to the wagon, and they were waiting at the door. Orville, Willie, and Cousin Beau stood in the muddy yard waving them off, but Cousin Mattie stayed inside. Even through the closed door they could hear the angry banging of pots and pans as she washed up after the meal.

Cousin Beau would really catch it later, thought Ginny, but at least she had Mama's shawl. She nestled in its folds, wishing that it still smelled of Mama's lavender instead of Cousin Mattie's camphor.

She was suddenly aware that the jolting wagon could not account for the heaving shoulders of the stranger next to her on the seat. As soon as they had driven a safe distance from the house, she understood. Mr. Mayhew was laughing. The laughter came from deep inside him, and now he let it loose in great, resounding roars.

"You and Beau sure give that old harridan her come-uppance," he declared. "I figured for sure she'd bust a corset string."

"You don't really think Mama gave her the shawl, do you?" asked Ginny.

" 'Course not," he assured her, between bursts of laughter. "It's yours all right. Just hope the rain won't hurt it none."

"I've seen Mama wear it in a shower," she told him. "But rain won't do my bonnet any good. I'd better take it off. I wouldn't want to spoil anything so pretty. Not after you went to all that trouble."

" 'Twasn't nothing," he said. But she had embarrassed him again, for he stopped laughing and clucked to the horses.

Ginny put the bonnet on her lap beneath the protecting folds of the shawl and sat up straight on the hard wooden wagon seat. In the excitement of securing her victory over Cousin Mattie she had almost forgotten where this journey was leading her. It was to a whole new way of life, a life for which she was unprepared. Mr. Mayhew was silent, too. He guided his team along the muddy road with great intensity.

The light mist soon gave way to heavy rain. It made a thick curtain that concealed the rolling hills to the distant right and rounded the tops of the trees that bordered LaCreole Creek on the left. On either side of the road were cleared acres of settlers' claims where only a few weeks before wheat and oats had stood high and glistening. Now the crops were harvested, and the stubble had been burned, a little trick the white settlers picked up from the Indians, who regularly burned over certain pasturage each fall. In the spring the wild grass came back thick and luxurious, and in the case of planted crops burning did away with some unwanted weeds.

Ginny stared at the acres of blackened ground without even knowing it was there. Her hair was plastered to her head and the folds of her shawl were growing sodden. She didn't even notice.

"I'm right sorry the wagon don't have no top," said Mr. Mayhew finally. "It was sunup when I left home, and the clouds hadn't blowed up. I had to take a wagon load of grain to Dallas, and I sort of figured it would be easier to drive on to Dixie afterwards. If I'd knowed the rain was going to come down like this, I'd have waited another day to fetch you."

"It doesn't matter," Ginny told him. He looked so

unhappy that she felt she ought to make some attempt at conversation. "Is Dallas near your land?"

"Little over three miles. You go to Dallas often?"

"I've never been there," she admitted. Dixie was only four miles from it, but Cousin Mattie saw no sense in gallivanting around when there was work to do at home.

"It's a nice little town," he assured her. "Growing, too. Got two general stores and a good blacksmith and wagonmaker and a cobbler and a saddle shop. John Maymire's got his gristmill there, but I use Jim Driscoll's on account it's closer."

"And a millinery store," prompted Ginny.

"That ain't a store exactly. Mis' Tolliver, she runs it in her house. Aunt Lizzie Davis told me about it. I guess you should rightly thank Aunt Lizzie for the bonnet. She told me I should buy it."

"Is she your aunt?" Ginny had never heard that Mr. Mayhew had any family.

"Aunt Lizzie's everybody's aunt," he told her, chuckling. "You'll find out when you meet her." Then his face grew serious. "Hope it won't be too lonesome for you. My place ain't like Dallas or even Dixie. Nearest neighbor's Jim Driscoll and he's a piece up the road."

"I'll be all right," said Ginny, but her tone must have lacked conviction, for he continued quickly.

"There's nothing to be skeered of. But if you should ever need it, I keep a loaded rifle hanging over the door in the kitchen."

Ginny nodded, and he went on speaking in the same anxious tone.

"I ain't met the new Mrs. Driscoll, but likely she'll

come calling. Her and Jim ain't been married too long. He used to have another wife, a Injun squaw, and I knowed her real good. Nice little thing, Nona was. But she went back to her tribe when Jim found himself a white woman that would marry him."

"Did he have trouble finding someone?" asked Ginny politely. She had heard that since the enactment of the Donation Land Claim Act there wasn't an unmarried woman in Oregon Territory.

"A mite." His eyes crinkled with amusement. "On account of his smell, most likely. Jim used to be a trapper in the old days. They didn't worry much about washing theirselves or their clothes. Maybe Jim promised to change. Anyway, he finally found somebody. Newcomer, up from by the Falls at Oregon City."

It was dark by the time they arrived at Mayhew's claim, and Ginny hoped her husband would think her shivering was caused by the cold rain, not by fear of him. He had done the best he could to make things easy for her.

"The team'll stand a minute," said Mr. Mayhew. "I'll build up the fire and get you some light. You best shuck out of them wet duds while I'm unhitching."

She followed him silently up a muddy path that led to a porch.

"Just finished the house this summer," he told her over his shoulder. "You likely won't remember, but I promised you a real house made out of planed lumber."

"I remember," Ginny agreed through chattering teeth.

"The old cabin where I used to live is out back." Suddenly he seemed filled with words, as though they might ease the tension they both felt. "I can use it for storing

28

things. The barn's out back, too. The well's over there to your right. And over there, though you can't see them, is four grafted apple trees. Henderson Luelling brung a wagonload across the plains in '49. I bought these off of him. I got the first apples this year and saved them for you."

"That's nice." Ginny heard her voice answering from what seemed a long way off.

Mr. Mayhew opened the door and hurried ahead. She heard familiar bangings, the kind Cousin Beau made when he poked up the fire each morning, and through the darkness a line of red appeared when the smoldering oak log was turned over. Mr. Mayhew threw on other wood, then leaned down to blow encouragingly. She could hear the popping of pitch as it caught, and in the growing light she saw her husband hold a long splinter in the flames and touch it to the wicks of several candles.

"There you are," he said cheerfully. "Make yourself to home. I'll be back soon as I seen to the stock." He slammed the door behind him as he went into the rainy night, leaving her there alone.

Ginny stood quietly, water dripping from her head and the edges of her shawl, looking around. The room was larger than the Danvilles' cabin and the walls were smooth lumber instead of rough logs. There was a table in the center, with four straight chairs pushed in around it, and a smaller table by the door. This held a water bucket, filled to the brim. There were cupboards built against one wall, containing an assortment of crockery and cooking pans, and a rocking chair stood by the fireplace.

But what held Ginny's eyes the longest was a

cookstove, a real cookstove, black iron, with an oven so bread didn't have to be baked in the fireplace or meats roasted on a spit. She hadn't even known there were stoves like this in Oregon. It must have come around the Horn in a sailing ship and probably cost a lot. Maybe her husband was old, but he must be rich, and he was doing everything he could to make her happy.

She took off the shawl and spread it over the rocker to dry, and placed the velvet bonnet carefully on the table. Then she went to investigate the stove more thoroughly, peering into the oven, lifting each of the four lids with an iron holder. The stove had never been used. It was waiting for her to be the first.

Suddenly she realized there was something missing in the room. A bed! There was no place to sleep! There were two closed doors besides the one they had used to enter. One must surely lead to the backyard, but what about the other? She crossed the clean board floor and turned the knob.

At first it was too dark to see, and she had to get a candle. The light shone on a bed covered with a bright patchwork quilt. It wasn't just a frame with legs set on the floor, either. It had its own head and footboards, made of a series of round wooden knobs. There was a matching bureau with a marble top and a real mirror. She set the candle on one of the little ledges provided for that purpose on either side of the glass and peered at her own reflection. Mercy, she did look a sight! It was the first time in years that she had seen herself, and she hoped that she would look better when she dried out.

There was a sudden bang and the candle flame fluttered in a gust of air. Ginny could hear Mr. Mayhew's feet on the wooden floor, and they sounded uneven as though he might be having trouble walking. The next minute he came through the bedroom door, and she hardly knew him. The blood had drained from his face, and it was greenish white.

"I—I got to lay down," he said, and toppled over on the bed.

chapter three

Ginny's chin sagged to her chest, and she woke with a start. There! She'd fallen asleep again, in spite of her firm resolve to stay awake. She didn't know how long she had slept, but the candle on the bureau had burned down to a pool of tallow and light was coming through the window. She felt stiff and tired after a night spent in one of the straight, hard chairs that she had brought from the other room, and she was cold as well. She hoped Mr. Mayhew was warm. At least he had stopped gasping and making those frightening sounds. She got up and made sure the coverings were tucked in about him securely.

It had been a terrible night. He had never roused after throwing himself on the bed, never spoken to her once. He just lay there, moaning and gasping for what seemed like hours. When he finally quieted, Ginny had pulled off his boots and doubled back the quilt and blanket so they would cover him. She had never been around anyone who was really sick, and she didn't know what else to do. But it didn't seem right for her to seek the warmth of the fire and leave him alone, so she had spent the long hours sitting in the unheated bedroom. Maybe he would open his eyes and tell her what was wrong.

Now that he seemed to be sleeping naturally was a good time to build up the fire. She had done it twice during the night, but it must need tending again. As she threw on the last of the wood, she realized that she would have to find the woodpile and bring in another load.

The back door opened into a small room like an enclosed porch. It was fitted with shelves, and here Mr. Mayhew had lined up his food supplies. A sack of flour, others of sugar, cornmeal, salt, a box of baking soda, and coffee beans beside their grinder. There was the tiny pile of apples that he had saved for her, eggs in a wooden box, and a bucket of milk with the cream risen to the top. The milk made her realize that there must be a cow in the barn, and the poor thing hadn't been attended to last night. That would have to be the first thing she did, even before bringing in wood.

She went back for her shawl, wishing that she had the old gray one as well as the paisley. It was too bad to wear anything so fine for milking, but it was all she had.

The rain had stopped during the night, and a pale blue

sky gave promise of a fine autumn day. The air smelled fresh and cold, and as she stood there inspecting the cluster of outbuildings, a gust of wind brought yellow oak leaves tumbling to the ground. The well was close to the house, and there was the old cabin Mr. Mayhew had lived in before building the new house. Near that was the slanting roof of a root cellar and a woodshed stacked high with a winter's supply. The barn was behind them all, with a fenced enclosure on one side. Mr. Mayhew was a good farmer, she decided, as well as a rich one. Everything was here that anyone could ask for. She should consider herself a lucky girl.

As her shoes squashed through the rain-soaked yard, she wondered why there were no noises from the barn. There should be protesting moos. Any cow used to twice-daily milking should be hurting by this time. Perhaps she was wrong. Perhaps Mr. Mayhew didn't own a cow and had bought the milk. But when she opened the door, there was a cow, regarding her with curious eyes but obviously in no discomfort.

Ginny pulled up the little three-legged stool and went to work. She could hear the horses snorting and moving around outside the stall, and she realized that she would have to throw down hay for them. She would have to feed the chickens, too. A rooster was calling to his hens some place outside. Mr. Mayhew would expect her to tend all the stock while he was sick. A farmer, or a farmer's wife, had to think of his animals before he thought of himself.

After the copious supply that Dolly yielded twice a day, this cow was a disappointment. There was only a scant bucket of milk, a regular milking. For a cow that had gone twenty-four hours it wasn't much. Ginny wondered if she should speak to Mr. Mayhew, when he was better, about getting a new cow. This one was hardly worth her feed.

Although she hurried, it took a little while to get everything done. When she finally returned to the house, Stephen Mayhew's eyes were open.

"I'm sorry," she told him breathlessly. "I did the milking. I threw down hay for the horses, too, and fed the chickens. I thought you were asleep."

He tried to smile, but his face was drawn.

"I'd better go to town for a doctor," she said. "I don't know what to do for you."

"I'll be fine." He spoke with difficulty. "Got me a pain in my chest. It'll go away."

"Would you like some breakfast?" She wanted to do something to help, and it was all she could think of.

"No. You eat. Go on, now."

Although she hadn't realized it before, she was hungry. It had been hours since that dinner at Cousin Beau's yesterday. Besides, she told herself as she ground coffee and stirred cornmeal into boiling water, maybe Mr. Mayhew would be hungry by the time it was ready.

But he still refused to eat even though she offered to spoon the mush into his mouth so he wouldn't have to sit up.

"Ginny." Every word seemed to be an effort. "If something happens—"

"Nothing's going to happen, Mr. Mayhew. You're going to be fine," she interrupted quickly, trying to keep

35

the fear from her voice. "You close your eyes and get some rest. I'm going to bring in more wood. What there was is all gone."

Once more she went outside, but this time she braved the chilly morning without a wrap. Goosebumps were preferable to snagging the paisley shawl on splintery wood.

It was while she was at the woodshed that she heard the horse. It was coming down the wagon trail that Mr. Mayhew had told her led to Jim Driscoll's claim. A horse meant a rider, someone who might be able to tell her what to do. She dropped the pile of wood she had gathered and ran out to the road.

"Stop! Stop!" she shrieked, and the rider pulled up his mount, staring down at her in surprise. He was a big man, dark, with a flowing beard that almost covered his face, and he wore a buckskin jacket trimmed with fringe.

"Please help me," she begged. "Mr. Mayhew's sick. I don't know what to do."

The man said something under his breath, but obediently turned off the road. Ginny followed, her dress accumulating splotches of mud thrown back by the horse's hooves.

"In here." She pushed ahead while the rider was dismounting and led the way.

There had been a change in the short time since she had gone for wood. Mr. Mayhew was breathing fast and irregularly, and the left side of his face seemed twisted out of shape.

"Old hoss," said the stranger, bending to touch the face on the pillow. "It's Driscoll. Can you hear me?"

"He looks worse," said Ginny in a frightened whisper. "I just left him for a minute."

"Reckon he's a goner," Driscoll told her bluntly. "I seed that look before. But happens I'm wrong, I'll fetch the doc."

Ginny trailed him to the door. Mr. Driscoll had been small comfort, although he had promised to hurry. But he wasn't hurrying now. Something had stopped him.

It was an Indian woman with a baby in a cradle board hanging down her back. She wore a long gray calico dress, with a skin robe around her shoulders, and she was holding fast to one of the stirrups that dangled from Driscoll's saddle.

"What you doing here, woman?" he shouted angrily. "I told you to pack moccasins and take the brat with you."

"Nona Jim Driscoll woman," insisted the Indian. "Papoose belong Jim Driscoll."

"I don't want you no more. Go back to your people. I got me a new woman. White woman. Married up with her in the church proper. Now you git."

He wrenched the stirrup from her hands and pushed her away so violently that she toppled into the mud.

Ginny stared open-mouthed, but neither one seemed aware that she was there. Jim Driscoll jumped into the saddle without bothering with stirrups and kicked his horse ahead, while the woman scrambled to her feet and ducked around the corner of the house. Ginny stared after her. Then she thought she heard a groan inside the house and hurried back to the bedroom.

Once more she resumed her vigil in the straight-backed chair beside the bed. Mr. Mayhew was still moaning, and she hoped he wasn't going to die. Mr. Driscoll had said he would, but so long as he kept breathing, there was hope. If only the doctor would get there, maybe he could do something.

The fire burned out because she had neglected to carry in the wood, but she didn't want to leave the sick man alone. She wrapped herself in the paisley shawl and wondered how long it would take for Mr. Driscoll to ride the three miles into town and return with help. It would depend on whether or not he could find the doctor. There was probably only one in town, and he might be out taking care of someone else. Mr. Mayhew might have to wait. She was so frightened that her own breath was coming in sharp gasps like that of the man on the bed.

It was noon before she heard wheels bumping through the ruts in front of the house. She was out of her chair in an instant and had the front door open before the high-wheeled buggy came to a stop.

There were two people on the single seat. The driver was a tall man with prematurely stooped shoulders and a lined face. He wore a black suit, shiny at the seat and bulging at each knee, and a flat, wide-brimmed hat. The passenger was a woman whose neat blue bonnet came only to the man's chest when he helped her from the vehicle. What she lacked in height she made up for in width, for under her blue shawl her body looked almost round. Her hair was gray, but her soap-shiny face was unwrinkled, and her eyes were as curious and friendly as a baby deer's.

"I'm Doc Boyle," called the man. "This here's Mrs.

Lizzie Davis. She happened to be at the house when Jim Driscoll stopped by, and she 'lowed as how she'd better come too. You'd be Mrs. Mayhew, I reckon?"

Ginny nodded shyly. It seemed strange to be called that by someone besides Orville and Willie, even though it had been her name for five years.

"You go right on in, Doc," urged Mrs. Davis. "Don't stall around wasting breath on being polite. It may be life or death. That's how Jim Driscoll put it and he should know, having seen plenty of it in his time."

Dr. Boyle took his bag from the floor of the buggy and hurried through the door while his companion followed more slowly. She had tiny feet and took short steps, so her progress was a little like a slow rolling ball.

"Now you tell Aunt Lizzie all about it," she urged, as soon as she had managed the two steps leading up to the porch. "What's it all about and when did it happen?"

There was something comforting in her voice. Ginny felt better just hearing it, as though here was someone prepared to take all her troubles on her own shoulders. She repeated her story, beginning with their arrival last night.

Mrs. Davis was a good listener. Her round eyes grew even rounder, and although she did not interrupt she kept up a series of clucking noises to show her sympathy and understanding.

"You poor lamb," she said, when Ginny finished. "What a wedding night. Not that it was your wedding exactly, but it was your first night in your new home that Stephen's been fixing up for so long. Well, there's nothing much we can do now but wait for Doc. Excepting I

39

do think we should build up that fire. You let it burn clean out."

"We're out of wood," explained Ginny. "I was getting some when Mr. Driscoll rode by, and then Mr. Mayhew seemed so bad I didn't like to leave him."

"Quite right, too. You're a good girl, Ginny. It is Ginny, ain't it? And I'm Aunt Lizzie. Wouldn't know who folks was talking to if they called me anything else."

"I'll go get the wood now," offered Ginny.

"While you're there, poke around where the chimney was built and see if you can't lay your hands on some loose bricks," Aunt Lizzie called after her. "Nothing like a hot brick wrapped in flannel to warm up sick folks' beds."

Ginny carried in an armload of wood, and while Aunt Lizzie was rekindling the fire, she went back to hunt for bricks and to fetch Aunt Lizzie's satchel, which was still in Dr. Boyle's buggy. They were both in the bedroom when she returned, but soon afterwards they came out.

"How is he?" she asked fearfully. Their faces were long and solemn.

"He's passed, poor soul," Aunt Lizzie told her sadly. "Gathered to his maker not five minutes past."

"A stroke," explained Dr. Boyle. "Wasn't nothing anybody could do."

"Not that you wasn't right to send for us," Aunt Lizzie put in hastily. "You poor child. A widow almost before you're a bride, and out here all alone with nobody to do for you."

"I'll get word to your folks," promised Dr. Boyle.

"That's all well and good for the burying tomorrow,"

agreed Aunt Lizzie. "It's proper they should be here for that, but they couldn't get here tonight, and the bereaved, she shouldn't be by herself. She can't tend to all the things that has to be done. I'm here now and here I intend to stay. Lucky Stephen ain't got no carpets yet, so we'll be saved the chore of taking them all up. But there's still a sight more that's got to be done. The mirror's got to be turned to the wall, and all the bedding in the house washed and hung out to dry in the wind. You know if Stephen's got baking sody, Ginny?"

Ginny nodded. She remembered seeing soda on the larder shelves.

"That's good," Aunt Lizzie approved. "Because we'll have to wring out rags in sody and water and keep changing them on his face the whole night through. We don't want to take a chance on his skin turning dark. We already put the pennies on his eyelids, you'll be glad to know."

Ginny stared at her, gulping a little. She couldn't believe this was happening. Not so much and in such a short time.

"You tell Tom Carson to send out a box for Stephen when you get back to town. He's got some already made up. It'll have to be a big one. Stephen was a big man." Aunt Lizzie had taken charge, and now she turned to address Dr. Boyle. "Then send around to Maria Heacock. Tell her we'd admire to borrow her black dress if it ain't too bad wore out, the one she had after Hank passed on. Ginny ain't got proper mourning clothes, have you, honey?"

Ginny shook her head mutely.

"Tell Maria to send the dress out with Tom when he brings the box," continued Aunt Lizzie. "And you better tell Pastor Seaforth early so he can start working on his sermon for Stephen. Pastor's getting old. Takes him a spell to figure things out these days. I reckon noon'd be the best time for the service. That way the stores can close up for the hour and the men folks can grab a bite before paying their respects. It'll give time for Ginny's folks to get here, too."

"Yes, ma'am," agreed Dr. Boyle calmly. "Anything else?"

"Not if you don't count seeing to somebody about digging Stephen's plot," she said thoughtfully. "I didn't mention that 'cause I knowed you'd tend to it without being told. And getting the word out to folks."

Dr. Boyle nodded again. Then he crossed the room and shook Ginny by the hand.

"I'm real sorry, Widow Mayhew," he said kindly. "Wished I could have helped. But I'll leave you in the best of hands. Aunt Lizzie will stay and see you through. She always does."

chapter four

"Now me and you better get to work," said Aunt Lizzie briskly as Dr. Boyle closed the door behind him. "Lucky there's a good wind. Noticed it when we was driving out here. It'll whip the bedding dry in no time."

"Yes, ma'am," agreed Ginny.

"We'll need water. Lots of it for all the wash we got to do, more than we can heat over the fireplace. We better fire up Stephen's stove, too."

"I'll get more wood," Ginny offered. "But I'll have to split some." She was glad now that Orville and Willie had sometimes neglected their chores and that she had

43

been forced to take over. There was a knack to splitting wood.

"Very good," approved Aunt Lizzie. To Ginny's disappointment she did not seem to think it strange that a young girl should be proficient in wood-splitting. "And after that you might fill all the kettles and pans you can find with wash water. I'll need some too. I'm going to lay out the body."

"Lay—" began Ginny, then stopped, suddenly aware that Aunt Lizzie was speaking of Mr. Mayhew.

"Yes, dearie," Aunt Lizzie told her. "It's got to be done, and I figure it's more fitting that I do it by myself. Poor Stephen's got to be washed all over, and while it's true that you're his widow, it's not quite the same as though you'd been living together. I hope you'll take kindly to the idea of my doing it alone. Though generally it takes two."

"Oh, yes," agreed Ginny quickly. She hoped Aunt Lizzie couldn't tell how relieved she was. "I think you're right. I'll get the wood right away."

As she left to go outside, Aunt Lizzie was pouring water from the bucket into the pot that hung from the crane. Her lips moved silently as she enumerated to herself the many things that must be done.

Stephen Mayhew's wood was easier to split than the supply Cousin Beau stored annually. This was under cover and dry, and there didn't seem to be quite so many knots. Moreover, he had a good-sized stack of kindling all prepared, and kindling was the hardest part. She carried the first armload inside and watched while Aunt Lizzie filled the cookstove. Ginny was glad she was there.

There was the matter of dampers to adjust for proper burning, something she knew nothing about.

She carried water from the well to fill all the containers they could find and left it heating while she went back for more wood. When she returned, Aunt Lizzie was secreted behind the closed door of the bedroom. In the middle of the floor was a great heap of blankets, sheets, and the patchwork quilt that had covered the bed. It was a mute reminder to start the laundry, so Ginny went back to the enclosed porch for a washtub, scrubboard, and a container of soft soap. Thanks to Cousin Mattie she knew how to do a washing, and she hoped that Aunt Lizzie wouldn't think boiling was necessary today.

"Not today," said Aunt Lizzie, in answer to Ginny's question about boiling. She had finally emerged, red-faced and perspiring, despite the chilliness of the bedroom. " 'Course, I know we should, but Stephen had his bedding clean as a hazel whistle on account of your coming. Neat and tidy, that man was. If we stop to boil, we'll never get things dry. Better hang it out quick as you can."

Mr. Mayhew had anticipated well, and there were clotheslines in the backyard. However, with such heavy articles as blankets, which took several clothespins to hold them in place, there was a shortage of pins. Ginny did the best she could and hoped the last blanket would hold with two.

When she went back inside, Aunt Lizzie was entertaining callers. One was their neighbor, Jim Driscoll, who sat uncomfortably on a straight-backed chair, the other was a woman whom Ginny rightly guessed to be his new wife.

Mrs. Driscoll was in her early thirties, a tall, bony woman with a long, somber face. Her brown hair was tightly screwed into a knot on the top of her head, and her eyes were small and darting. Although there was no physical resemblance, there was something about her that reminded Ginny of Cousin Mattie.

"Jim and Mrs. Driscoll stopped by to pay their respects," explained Aunt Lizzie, who had appropriated the rocker beside the fire. "She brung you a dish of baked beans."

"It was all I had cooked up," apologized Mrs. Driscoll. "Jim brung the news so sudden there was no time to fix a pie."

"Nobody ever turned up their nose at good baked beans," Aunt Lizzie told her graciously. "We're much beholding."

"Yes. Thank you." Ginny took a third chair, the one closest to Jim Driscoll, then wished she hadn't. There was certainly a peculiar smell about him, just as Mr. Mayhew had warned. Since he looked comparatively clean, she decided the odor must be clinging to his leather jacket.

"It's sad," said Mrs. Driscoll, "to be took so sudden. No warning at all, I reckon?"

"Nary a bit." Aunt Lizzie shook her head. "Took in his prime of life, Stephen was. You might say just as his life was about to begin."

Since Aunt Lizzie seemed both capable and willing to carry on the conversation, Ginny let her. She was a little glad that the arrival of callers had given her a chance to rest. She had slept but little the night before, and she was very tired. The talk flowed about her, and she hardly heard what was being said. Then in a sudden silence, she was aware that everyone was looking at her.

"I'm sorry," she stammered. "You said—"

"I asked what you aimed to do," repeated Mrs. Driscoll disapprovingly. "Now that your husband's gone, you aim to stay on here or move back with your folks?"

"Oh, no," cried Ginny in alarm. "I won't go back. I'll stay here."

"It's her right," said Jim Driscoll gloomily. "All this belongs to her now. To a slip of a girl. And I don't blame her for sitting on it."

The Driscolls left soon after that. Aunt Lizzie and Ginny saw them to the door, thanking them again for their call.

"Jim, he didn't get no prize in that one," pronounced Aunt Lizzie, as they drove away. "But then, she didn't neither. I wonder if her beans is fit to eat. Too bad we didn't have nothing to offer them. I did say I'd make coffee, and I was some relieved when they didn't want none. Still we best get some mourning meat of our own on to cook."

"Mourning meat?"

"So we can offer callers a bite of something. Not that we're likely to have many callers this far from town, but you never know. Why don't you see what Stephen's got? His meathouse ain't built yet, so you'll likely find it in the root cellar or else in his old cabin. Get a ham, if he's got one, or a haunch of beef."

47

The root cellar was closer to the house, so Ginny tried that first. Sure enough, there were two hams hanging from a supporting beam and almost a whole side of beef. There were also potatoes, onions, carrots, parsnips, and squash stored tidily in gunnysacks.

As she went by the clothes line, she felt the blankets and was relieved to find that they were drying fast in the gusty wind. By nightfall she could bring them in.

Aunt Lizzie parboiled the ham in a kettle of water to remove the surplus salt, then lifted the dripping meat by two forks into a pan, and plopped it into the oven of the stove.

"We'll need more wood, Ginny," she said, with a glance at the now nearly depleted woodbox.

Wearily, Ginny went back to the woodshed. By this time she was so tired she could hardly swing the axe.

"You look tuckered," said Aunt Lizzie, when she returned to the overheated house. A fire in the fireplace and another in the stove made the small room unbearably hot. "Set a spell. I'll just finish sweeping up this floor, then maybe a cup of tea would go down good for both of us."

But there was no time to make tea, for a wagon drove into the muddy yard before Aunt Lizzie had finished sweeping.

"It's Tom Carson with Stephen's box," announced the lady, hurrying to peer out of one of the uncurtained windows. "And Pastor Seaforth, too. Ginny, honey, maybe you ought to change your dress. The one you're wearing is pretty dirty, especially around the skirt."

"I can't," Ginny told her. "This is all I've got."

48

"I mean to an everyday dress," explained Aunt Lizzie kindly. "Even clean calico's better than dirty muslin that you wore for two days. This is the preacher coming."

"I don't have another dress," explained Ginny again. "This is all I came with."

Aunt Lizzie's blue eyes grew even rounder, and for once she seemed at a loss for words. Her mouth opened and closed several times, but nothing came out.

There were sounds of feet on the porch before she finally recovered herself enough to open the door.

"Come in, Pastor," she invited. "And Tom. This is the Widow Mayhew. Poor little thing, she's been through a sight since she come, as you can see for yourself just by looking at her. Ain't even had time to put herself to rights."

Pastor Seaforth was small and stooped. When he removed his hat, his bald head glistened in the late afternoon sunlight coming through the western windows. He took Ginny's hand, and it felt like holding a fluttering bird, but his wrinkled face was kind.

"Our deepest sympathy, Widow Mayhew." His voice was amazingly loud. "We do not know why these things happen, but the Lord moves in strange ways His wonders to perform. In good time all things will be made known to us."

After the minister's limp handshake, Tom Carson's vigorous pumping was something of a shock. He was a big man, with burly shoulders and weathered skin. He never addressed her directly, but from time to time she caught him studying her curiously.

"I didn't expect to see you, Pastor." Aunt Lizzie raised

her voice whenever she spoke to him, so Ginny decided he must be hard of hearing. "What with tomorrow's sermon and all."

"It is my Christian duty to call upon the sick and bereaved," he told her promptly. "Besides, my nephew Gilbert, whom we've been expecting for so long, arrived on the early stage. I set him to work at once. Tomorrow's service will be a good opportunity for the townspeople to hear him."

"You mean your nephew's finally got out of preaching school? You been talking about him so long I never did think to lay eyes on that young man," Aunt Lizzie admitted.

"It takes more than a few months to complete the studies, Mrs. Davis," he told her. "But Gilbert has mastered it in the best tradition. I asked him to come here first, so my friends might judge him. I am no longer a young man. God will be calling me soon, and—"

"Pshaw, Pastor," she interrupted. "You got years yet. Not that folks won't be glad to listen to your nephew, of course, and Stephen's burying is a good time. Even the members that don't come regular will be there tomorrow. Tom, you bring the box? You sure it's big enough?"

"I brung the *coffin*, Aunt Lizzie," Tom corrected her indignantly. "And it's plenty big. I guess I knowed Stephen as well as you."

"And Maria's black dress?"

"She was glad to send it. She sent along some fresh baked bread, too, and some preserves, being as how she couldn't call personal. And Miranda sent a pie. She'd just baked it for our supper, but she 'lowed this was a better use."

50

"She's quite right," approved Aunt Lizzie. "Stephen's in here if you want to pay your respects."

Ginny sat down again as they all trooped into the bedroom. She was thankful for Aunt Lizzie, who was willing to take care of everything. Obviously no one expected Ginny to do anything. A little guiltily, she glanced at the woodbox and was relieved that it was still partially full.

After a few minutes Stephen's friends returned to the kitchen. Pastor Seaforth sat with Ginny and in a voice that he was obviously trying to keep low quoted scriptures. She gave him only part of her attention as she watched Tom Carson carry a long wooden box into the bedroom. He and Aunt Lizzie spent some time in there. Afterwards he brought in various parcels and bundles from the wagon, but before he and the minister left he went back outside. Through the walls Ginny could hear the sound of an axe and she knew he was chopping wood. She was especially thankful for that.

When the men left, Aunt Lizzie decided it was time for supper. She insisted that she prepare it by herself.

"Nothing to making tea and slicing ham and Maria's bread," she explained. "I could do it in my sleep. 'Tain't like we was in town. There folks would have the room overflowing with food, but there's plenty here for me and you."

While they were eating, she suddenly remembered something. From her apron pocket she produced ten twenty-dollar gold pieces and dropped them on the table beside Ginny's teacup.

"Found them in Stephen's pants pocket," she explained. "Likely what he got in town for his wheat."

Two hundred dollars! Ginny had never seen so much money before in her life.

"It's yours," Aunt Lizzie assured her. "It'll take one of them to pay for the burying tomorrow, what with Tom Carson and the diggers and Pastor Seaforth's nephew, but that still leaves you something to get along on."

Ginny shook her head speechlessly.

"I been thinking," continued Aunt Lizzie delicately, "that you should buy some yard goods and get Rebecca Tolliver to make you up some dresses. Black, of course, since you'll be in mourning for a year. The one Maria Heacock sent is all very well for tomorrow, but it's considerable worn. Maybe you should tend to that before you go back to your cousin's place."

"But I told you," cried Ginny loudly. "I'm not going back there. Not ever."

Aunt Lizzie looked at her with troubled eyes but did not answer.

They both dozed sitting in chairs before the fire throughout the night. At intervals they roused themselves to wring cloths out of baking soda and water to exchange for those already covering Stephen Mayhew's face and hands. Since they had no clock, Ginny was not sure this was done every half hour as prescribed, but it did seem that they made many trips into the bedroom. At first she was a little afraid, but she soon forgot her fears. Mr. Mayhew looked contented lying there in Tom Carson's box. The red flush had faded from his face, but that could have been candlelight. He seemed to be smiling at her, telling her that everything was going to be all right. She wished he didn't have to have those pennies,

52

each as big as fifty-cent pieces, on each eyelid, but Aunt Lizzie assured her they were necessary. Otherwise, she said, the eye muscles might relax and they would find Stephen staring into their faces.

When daylight began creeping through the windows, Aunt Lizzie came to with a start.

"Sakes alive!" she cried. "Here we are, sleeping through the morning and us with so much to do. And the fire's near gone out, too."

Ginny, who had finally curled up on the floor on the pile of freshly washed blankets, awoke suddenly. For a minute she thought she was back at Cousin Beau's and it was time to start her chores.

"The cow!" she exclaimed. "I've got to milk the cow."

"Cow! Oh, the poor critter," said Aunt Lizzie compassionately. "She wasn't milked last night either. You take care of that, Ginny, and I'll stir up the fire and see to breakfast."

Both milk pails were still full so Ginny ruthlessly emptied the contents of one on the ground. She could see no churn, so there was little use in saving butterfat. The important thing was to relieve the suffering cow.

But once again the cow seemed to be in no discomfort, and the yield was the same as yesterday morning.

"You really aren't worth much," Ginny told her as she finished. "I wish I had Dolly here. She'd show you what a cow ought to do."

It was going to be another clear day. The sky was pale blue with a fading crescent of moon still visible in the west. Then Ginny saw something else, something that made her catch her breath in horror. A thin sliver of

53

smoke was coming from the chimney of the old log cabin back of the new house. Fire must have started inside.

Still grasping her pail of milk she raced for the cabin. For a minute the door resisted her efforts, then it fell back heavily. The single room was dark with shadows, but there was enough light to see someone bending over the fireplace. There were no longer flames, only sputtering embers, but in their light Ginny caught a metallic gleam that could have been a knife in the person's hand.

"You tell, I kill you," said a threatening voice from the shadows.

chapter five

Ginny's first impulse was to run. Then she realized that the threatening voice was not that of a man. It was a woman, probably a young woman. Most likely it was the Indian girl she had seen yesterday.

"You used to be Jim Driscoll's wife, didn't you?" she asked. "What was it Mr. Mayhew called you? Nona?"

The woman did not answer, and Ginny tried again.

"How long have you been hiding in this cabin?"

"You tell, I kill," repeated Nona sullenly. "Stephen Mayhew not care Nona here."

By now Ginny's eyes were beginning to adjust to the gloom. The metallic gleam, which she had mistaken for a knife, was a tin milk bucket. Nona had been using its contents to put out the fire that she had only dared burn at night. There was no furniture in the room, but on the hearth was a bulky blanket-wrapped bundle.

"How long have you been hiding here, Nona?" she asked gently.

The Indian woman shrugged. Time was of no importance.

"Did Mr. Mayhew know you were here?"

There was still no answer.

"Mr. Mayhew died, Nona. He's going to be buried today."

"You lie." There was a note of alarm in the voice from the shadows. "Whites all lie to Nona. Jim Driscoll lie."

"Did you go back to your tribe?"

"Nona take baby. Visit. Come back. Wait. Soon Jim Driscoll tire of white squaw. Tell her go away. Take Nona back."

"I don't think it's going to happen that way," Ginny told her regretfully. "I think he'll keep his white wife."

"Nona wait," she insisted stubbornly.

"Well, you can stay here. At least for a while," decided Ginny thoughtfully. "I think Mr. Mayhew would want you to. What do you have to eat?"

"Spuds." Nona kicked indifferently at something on the hearth. "Milk for baby."

"You've been milking the cow! At night when I forgot." So that accounted for the small yield and the lack of the cow's discomfort. "I'm glad you did, Nona. We're going to be gone all day. When we leave, you can come out and even build up your fire if you want to. But you'd better put it out in the late afternoon before we get back. And bar the door."

Nona did not reply, but Ginny knew she was listening.

"I'll leave some bread and meat just outside the back door. When you see us drive away, you can get it. We'll have to figure out later what to do." She closed the door behind her, and after a minute she heard the heavy bar fall into place.

Aunt Lizzie had breakfast waiting by the time she returned to the house, and Maria Heacock's black dress was spread out on a chair. It was really very ugly, Ginny decided, but at least it was clean. She put it on with the brown velvet bonnet and the paisley shawl. Aunt Lizzie was disturbed about the colors since mourning clothes should be strictly black. But she agreed they would have to do.

"Folks will understand," she said. "Stephen being took so sudden and all, you've got to wear what's to hand."

Tom Carson drove up soon after that with another man. They hoisted Stephen's casket into the back of the wagon. It would go straight to the church, while Aunt Lizzie and Ginny would follow in the light buggy, which was stored in the barn next to the heavy farm wagon.

"We'll go to my house," announced Aunt Lizzie. "I can get myself ret up there and fix a bite for us before the service. Josiah and Jeth will come home early from the shop, and folks can stop in and pay their respects afterwards."

"Josiah and Jeth?" For some reason Ginny had never thought that Aunt Lizzie might have a family of her own.

"Josiah's my husband. Owns the saddle shop in town. Jeth's my nephew. Took him to raise when his ma, my only sister, passed on with lung fever. His father was took soon after. Me and Josiah never had no young 'uns, so it's been a comfort having a boy around the house. Josiah, he's teaching Jeth the trade, since it'll all be his some day. Not that he takes to the work much, but you know how boys are."

Ginny agreed absently. Her mind was more concerned with the Indian woman in the cabin than with small boys. She hoped Nona would find the bread and meat she had left on the back step.

"Aunt Lizzie, do you have many Indians around here?" she asked, wincing as the horse stepped carefully around a pothole in the road, dragging the buggy wheels through it.

"A few." A look of real dislike erased the pleasant expression on the round, shiny face. "They come begging around the stores sometimes, and the squaws come to the doors trying to sell baskets or berries. But the prices they ask! A dime for a basket and two bits for a gallon of wild blackberries. Not that it ain't hard work picking them, but two bits! Why, when I was young—"

"Mr. Driscoll used to be married to one, didn't he?" Ginny was determined that Aunt Lizzie shouldn't go wandering off on another subject.

"Reckon so," she agreed, pursing her lips in disapproval. " 'Course, he wasn't married in a church, though they might have had some kind of heathen ceremony for all I know. Folks in town never seen her, and she's gone now that he finally found hisself a real wife."

"Why didn't they see her? Didn't she ever come to town?"

"Not likely," denied Aunt Lizzie, sniffing. "Jim

wouldn't hear of it. He knowed how folks felt. You mustn't let a Injun in your house, Ginny. They'd steal you blind every time. But I don't think you need to worry. Ain't no Injun villages out where you live. You're safe enough. If you should see one, just take down Stephen's gun and wave it around a bit. The Injun will skedaddle."

Ginny didn't reply.

When they drove over the covered bridge spanning the LaCreole, Ginny looked around with interest. This was the first time she had been in Dallas. Although it was the county seat, there was not too much to see. It consisted of one main street two blocks long, with a few business houses on each side. The residences were scattered in the fields behind, and Aunt Lizzie directed her to turn the horse into a muddy road that led to the right.

The Davis residence was built of logs. It was one story but had obviously been added onto from time to time so that it rambled over a considerable area. There were the remains of flower beds in front, with a vegetable garden behind, beside the barn.

"Not much in the way of posies left to take to the burying," observed Aunt Lizzie, frowning as they drove up to the door. "Few little asters, but likely the rain's spoiled them when you get up close. But I brung in my geraniums early, and they was blooming when I left. I'll pick them off for Stephen."

A tall young man came outside as Ginny signaled the horse to stop. He wore a blue flannel shirt with rough brown trousers, and his sandy hair stuck up in a cowlick. Ginny was not used to young men and she looked at him curiously. He had round blue eyes and pink cheeks like Aunt Lizzie's, and the pink spread higher on his face as he saw her staring at him.

"My nephew, Jeth Manning." Aunt Lizzie introduced them briskly. "He'll take your rig around to the barn. This is the Widow Mayhew, Jeth."

Jeth ducked his head and mumbled something as he helped them from the seat. Ginny was surprised. The way Aunt Lizzie had spoken, she had imagined Jeth was a little boy. She was unprepared for someone her own age. Older perhaps. Jeth could be seventeen or eighteen.

Aunt Lizzie ushered her straight into the cabin. They were in a room which doubled as kitchen and living room, for there were two cushioned rockers in front of the fireplace and pots and pans and bunches of drying herbs hanging from the ceiling. A smiling little man, who was almost the duplicate in size of Aunt Lizzie, arose from one of the rockers and came forward with hand extended. This was her husband, Josiah Davis. After a moment his welcoming smile dissolved as he remembered it was a solemn occasion.

"Well," said Aunt Lizzie, turning to survey the table in the center of the room. It was covered with food of all kinds—cakes, pies, bread, cooked meat, jars of preserves and jellies, pickles and covered dishes at whose contents Ginny could not guess.

"Folks been sending it over since last night, soon as the word got out," explained Josiah. "Me and Jeth was some tempted, too, I might add."

"I hope you put temptation behind you," Aunt Lizzie told him severely. "This is for the bereaved and them that calls to pay their respects, as you very well know.

Ginny, honey, shuck off your shawl and bonnet while I get ret up. Then we best put something in our stomachs before folks start dropping in."

"Shucks, Lizzie," protested Josiah. "They won't drop in till afterwards. There's plenty of time."

"No, there ain't," she denied. "And when he gets back, tell Jeth to shed them work clothes. He can't go to a burying looking like that."

Ginny took off her bonnet and shawl and accepted the rocker opposite Josiah. After what he considered a proper inteval of mournful silence, the crinkly smile returned to his eyes and mouth.

"You're a mighty pretty girl," he said approvingly. "Though black don't become you. You need pretty colors."

"I don't like black either," she admitted shyly.

"Only thing you can do is pick yourself out a new husband," he told her. "Out here, where ladies is scarce, folks look the other way after six months of mourning. Naturally, it wouldn't be respectful to go on mourning your old husband when you got a new one."

"No, I guess it wouldn't," agreed Ginny. She found herself smiling back at him. It was good to be in this house with these kindly people. All her past unhappiness seemed to melt away.

Jeth returned from stabling the horse and was given his aunt's message. Without a word he left the room, presumably to get into his Sunday clothes. He was a very shy young man, Ginny decided. It was too bad he hadn't inherited some of his aunt and uncle's outgoing qualities.

Before long there was a knock at the door, and to

Ginny's surprise it proved to be Julia Bridges accompanied by a strange man.

"Julia Gates now," she explained smugly. "This is my husband, Henry. We were married last summer. Maybe you heard. Henry owns the general store. Ginny was my dearest friend, for a year anyway, while I went to Mr. Lyle's school in Dixie," she explained to Josiah. "This is terrible, Ginny, this awful thing that's happened to you."

Aunt Lizzie returned, rustling a little in her black dress with a hair brooch at the throat. She hadn't realized that Julia Gates and Ginny were acquainted, and there was much to-do about the fact.

"Henry says I'm not a very good cook yet," admitted Julia, glancing at the loaded table, "so he said I'd better not try to bake. We brought you some coffee and some sugar because I remember you never got as much sugar as you wanted on your mush, Ginny."

"Hm," said Aunt Lizzie, regarding the two paper-wrapped bundles that Henry Gates had placed on the table. "Looks about two pounds of sugar, Henry, and is that a pound of coffee?"

"Half pound," he told her stiffly. "You can mix it with chicory. Coffee's very dear now. Shipping rates and all."

After that, more guests arrived and there was such a rush there was no time for anyone to eat. Aunt Lizzie suggested cutting some of the pies or cakes on the table, but everyone said no. They'd finished dinner before they left home. Better leave the food until afterwards. It would give them something to look forward to.

Finally Josiah produced a huge watch from his pocket

62

and announced that it was time they were leaving for the church.

"Your folks ain't here, honey," whispered Aunt Lizzie anxiously. "Want us to wait a little longer?"

"No." Ginny tried to keep the relief from her voice. "Maybe somebody was sick and they can't come."

"Then me and Josiah and Jeth will be with you," replied Aunt Lizzie. "And act as family."

But she spoke too soon, for when they reached the church, a small building painted white and topped by a cupola still waiting for a bell, the Danville family occupied the front pew. Cousin Beau rose courteously when he saw Ginny to allow her to slide in between him and Cousin Mattie.

Ginny sat down on the hard seat and felt her eyes fill with tears. She knew it was all right. People would think she was crying for Stephen Mayhew, but really it was because she had found herself surrounded by her cousins again. Just as she had thought herself free of them, here they were. And she knew all too well what that meant.

Through blurred eyes she stared straight ahead at the long box, surmounted by a cheery bunch of Aunt Lizzie's geraniums, and at the simple altar beyond. But as she stared, the tears dried and she wiped them away quickly. The most beautiful man she had ever seen had just taken his place behind the pulpit.

He was tall, with black hair that waved from a pale forehead. No farmer's weatherbeaten skin for Pastor Gilbert Seaforth. He had large eyes, although from this distance Ginny could not tell if they were brown or gray. His features were clean and regular. His white collar was immaculate and the shoulders of his black coat fitted perfectly. The hands with which he grasped each side of the pulpit were white, not hardened with work callouses. Moreover, he was just the right age, no more than twenty-five.

Even before he spoke, she knew how his voice would sound, and it did not disappoint her. It was deep and rich and cultured. Although it had been so long ago, she was sure the voices of the gentlemen in Carolina had sounded that way. True, he didn't have a southern accent like the men in Dixie, but there was no mistaking the fact that he was a gentleman. She listened, enraptured by his voice, without bothering to heed the words, and she was glad that the sermon was so long. Behind her, some of the mourners fidgeted with impatience, but Ginny could have sat on and on.

Once she reminded herself that it was sinful to be thinking of Pastor Gilbert Seaforth when her thoughts should be of Stephen Mayhew. But she couldn't help herself. She went on thinking of him anyway.

Finally it was over. The choir sang a mournful song, and the congregation filed by for a last glimpse of their friend. Ginny lingered a moment, saying a silent thank-you to the kind man who lay there quietly sleeping. Then Cousin Mattie's sharp fingers in her arm hurried her along.

As yet the town had no hearse, so Tom Carson's wagon again transported the casket to the cemetery at the edge of town. Almost everyone followed, and Cousin Beau's wagon was at the front in line. For once Ginny did not have to ride in back with Orville and Willie, but she wished it had been possible. The seat was made for two, and she was squeezed in between Cousin Beau and Cousin Mattie. Only one exchange of remarks was made on the way.

"A paisley shawl's not fitting for a widow," said Cousin Mattie. "I'll knit you a black one."

"No, you won't," objected Ginny sharply. "It's my shawl and I'll wear it." She wished that Stephen Mayhew could hear her. She knew he would approve.

As she watched the long box being lowered into the ground, Ginny felt her throat tighten. The last time she had witnessed such a thing had been on the Platte. Then it had been her mother and father who were swallowed by the earth. She had known Mr. Mayhew only a few hours, but he had been kind. She mourned him now, just as his many friends were mourning him.

Afterwards Pastor Seaforth and his nephew came up to her, the first with his fluttery-bird handshake and Gilbert with hands that were smoother than her own.

"Be brave, Widow Mayhew," boomed Pastor Seaforth. "Stephen is with his maker now."

"My uncle and I will call on you in a few days," promised Gilbert. He looked deep into her eyes and his, she was pleased to learn, were hazel. "Just to see how you are bearing up."

"Folks have sent their vittles to our house," said Aunt Lizzie, hurrying over and addressing Cousin Mattie. "Since Ginny didn't live in town, they didn't know where else to send them. We'll be pleased for you to stop."

"Oh, yes," agreed Cousin Mattie. "We'll stop."

But once they stopped, they did not linger, although the room was rapidly filling with people.

"Beau, you and the boys carry all that food out to the back of the wagon," ordered Cousin Mattie, after she had inspected the crowded table. "And you young 'uns, watch that you don't put your feet in nothing."

"But I figured you'd stay on a spell," protested Aunt Lizzie. "Meet the folks and all."

"No time," said Cousin Mattie. "They tell me it's a good three mile out to Mr. M—to Ginny's place, and the road's probably chuck-a-block with holes. We better get on. Thank you kindly, everybody."

Ginny looked at Aunt Lizzie, who seemed about to cry. She walked over and put her arms around the plump figure.

"I'm sorry," she whispered. "She's always like this. I was too ashamed to tell you. Thank you for everything."

She smiled apologetically at the circle of astonished faces about the now-emptied food table. They were all too confused to acknowledge her smile except Jeth. He seemed to have lost his shyness. Now he was grinning widely, and when he caught her eye, he gave a deliberate wink. She ignored him and followed the Danvilles out the front door.

chapter six

*I*t wouldn't have hurt to stay around a bit and be sociable, Mattie," protested Cousin Beau. They were driving through the covered bridge at the edge of town, and the wooden sides gave his voice an echoing quality. "They looked like good folks, and they only wanted to be nice."

"They just came to fill their gullets," Cousin Mattie told him snappishly. "I don't hold with making a party out of somebody's dying. Maybe they pretended that stuff was meant for Ginny, but you can bet your boots they aimed to eat their share and more. But we outfoxed them good."

Ginny, who had now been relegated to the wagon box along with Orville and Willie, looked at the assortment of food, which had been carefully deposited on the floor. There was far more than she and the Danvilles could ever eat. Cakes and pies would dry up, probably untasted, and whatever was in the covered dishes would doubtless spoil. Moreover, Cousin Mattie had made enemies. What she had done would be talked about for a long time, and some of the criticism would fall on Ginny herself.

"What's Mr. Mayhew's house like?" asked Willie curiously. "Is it big?"

"Bigger than yours," she told him shortly.

"Ma said Mr. Mayhew was rich," reported Orville. "And all his money goes to us now."

Of late Ginny had tried to avoid looking at her young cousins. It was better to ignore them. But now she glared at Orville with an expression of loathing. Really, he was the most repulsive little boy, with his thin hair slicked back with a little lard to make sure it stayed in place for his public appearance at the funeral. Every day he grew to look more and more like his mother, and his voice, as he repeated the words, had been an exact imitation of hers, too. She wished she dared slap him across his grinning face, but she had never been allowed to lay a hand on the boys.

"It goes to me," she said fiercely, remembering the gold pieces she had placed in the sugar bowl on the kitchen shelf. She would transfer them to a safer place the minute they arrived.

"You're only a girl," Orville said. "You don't count.

Pa's your living relative. It's his duty to look after things for you."

"Not any more. I'm married now." But as she spoke, Ginny wondered if she were right. She wasn't sure what the law would say about it. Maybe Orville was telling the truth. Still Aunt Lizzie had given the gold pieces to her. She hadn't waited for Cousin Beau and turned them over to him. And Jim Driscoll had said the farm belonged to Stephen Mayhew's widow. There had been a little envy in his voice, but there was a tinge of truth, too.

"You was married before, but it didn't count," Orville reminded her. He tried to continue the argument, but Ginny refused to say any more. She sat silently, staring over the sides of the wagon, and after a while Orville gave up.

The wagon jolted and bumped, but she hardly noticed the discomfort. She was too miserable for that. She sat with her legs, concealed by Maria Heacock's long black skirt, stretched straight ahead and tried to ignore everyone in the wagon. She deadened her ears to the bickering of Orville and Willie, the shouted orders of Cousin Mattie to keep their fingers out of the whipped cream frosting cake, and Cousin Beau's running comments on the countryside. Life was so unfair. Just as she thought she'd made a friend, something happened to snatch him away. Mr. Mayhew had been a friend. Look at the house he had built and the comforts he had installed just for her. Aunt Lizzie had been a friend, and Josiah would have been. Maybe even Jeth. That wink as they were leaving might have meant that he sympathized with her embarrassment. The townspeople she had met

69

so briefly seemed friendly, but if she ever saw them again they wouldn't be. Cousin Mattie had spoiled all that.

"Ginny! Your Cousin Beau asked you a question!" Cousin Mattie's voice broke into her thoughts.

"I just asked if Mr. Mayhew's land didn't start somewhere around here," called Cousin Beau.

They had come to a stand of heavy timber. Trees had been cleared to make a narrow road between giant firs that rose towering in the air.

"It's the beginning of his land," Ginny reported, remembering that Aunt Lizzie had told her so just that morning.

"Stephen planned on clearing this out some day," she had said. "But he didn't figure there was no hurry. When you take a Donation Land Claim, some of the six hundred and forty acres has got to be left in timber, but clearing out the rest of it takes time. Stephen had plenty of cleared land to start on."

Ginny was glad that Mr. Mayhew hadn't got around to clearing all the trees. They weren't like the crowded growth that Cousin Beau kept saying he was going to fell and never did. These were well-spaced so the trunks had grown to be several feet across, and they were a little like an army of warriors standing guard. In summer it would be cool beneath their scented branches, and in the winter those same branches would offer protection for the wild things of the forest when the snow lay heavy in the clearing.

She had not been aware of the trees on the night of her arrival. Then it had been dark, and perhaps she had been too nervous. But this morning she had heard the wind rustling in the high branches like a whispered song, perhaps a final farewell to the man who was leaving them for the last time.

The wind was blowing again this afternoon. The tree tops kept moving and bending with a steady sibilant sound that was almost threatening. The ground below was strewn with small twigs that had been whipped from larger branches.

"Hurry up that team, Beau," Cousin Mattie ordered with a shiver. "I shouldn't care to have one of these monsters fall on me."

"Don't reckon there's much danger," said Cousin Beau. "Likely they've seen worse winds than this." But he clucked to his horses obediently.

But if Cousin Mattie didn't approve of the forest, she did of the house.

"Not bad," she conceded when Cousin Beau pulled up at the front door. "Better than ours by a long sight."

"Planed lumber. Looks to be nice and tight, too," agreed Cousin Beau admiringly. "All it needs is paint. You go on in. The boys'll help me see to the team."

"You leave the team right here till we unpack those vittles," ordered Cousin Mattie. "You young 'uns, watch that you don't stick your fingers in the frosting on the cakes. I don't want finger-licking going on."

She climbed down from the seat and mounted the two steps, pausing to jiggle a moment on each one to make sure it was secure. The others followed more slowly. By the time Ginny arrived, carrying a burnt-sugar cake in one hand and a custard pie in the other, Cousin Mattie was standing in the center of the kitchen, her eyes taking inventory of everything.

"A real cookstove at last," she said appreciatively. "Let's hope it don't smoke."

She opened the bedroom door and went inside. Ginny could hear her moving around, making little comments as she opened bureau drawers and turned the mirror around to its proper place.

"Come on, Mrs. Mayhew," said Orville. "Just 'cause you're a married lady, you can't get out of your share of toting."

Ginny obediently went back to the wagon for more food. Whatever will we do with it, she wondered. The table was smaller than Aunt Lizzie's, and it was already full. By the time they had finished stacking the remainder on shelves, Cousin Mattie had completed her tour of the bedroom. She had also briefly inspected the enclosed back porch and peered into the back yard.

"This is going to be lots better, Beau," she reported. " 'Course, there's things to be done, but we'll be comfortable here. And that bed, you'll be glad to know, has a real feather tick. We won't be sleeping on straw. There's a mirror to the bureau, too, and drawers to store things. Time the cold weather sets in, we'll be snug as a bug."

"Where do we sleep?" demanded Willie. "Ain't no loft here."

"That's one of the drawbacks," admitted his mother. "You and Orville, and of course Ginny, will have to have pallets here on the floor. But it'll be nice and warm in front of the fire. Beau, I figure you should drive home tomorrow and see about renting our place. It'll take a little while, probably, but we'll make out just fine till you get back."

Ginny heard her with growing anger. This was her house. Mr. Mayhew had built it for her. He had told her so. He didn't even like Cousin Mattie. He had called her an old harridan, and he wouldn't want her moving in and sleeping in his fine bed and cooking on his new stove and taking over as though it belonged to her.

"I won't sleep on the floor," she said defiantly. "The bedroom is mine."

"Nonsense!" Cousin Mattie objected. "I never heard such talk. You certainly can't expect your Cousin Beau and me to sleep on the floor. After all we've done for you."

"I expect you to go home," Ginny told her. "Back to your place in Dixie. The place you bought with the money you got for selling me."

"That'll be quite enough," declared Cousin Mattie. In the old days she would have sent Ginny to her corner behind the curtain, but here there was no place to send her but the bedroom. And she didn't want to send her there.

"Ginny, honey." Cousin Beau began placatingly, but she cut him short.

"I'm a married woman now. My husband built this house for me. He told me so. And you can't try to move in and take it away from me just because he died. It's mine. You've got no business being here without an invitation. And I didn't invite you."

"Ginny, honey, we're your family," Cousin Beau reminded her. "You can't stay here alone."

"Who says I'll be alone? Aunt Lizzie will find some-body to stay with me. I know she will."

"You're a selfish, ungrateful baggage, that's what you are!" Cousin Mattie accused angrily. "And I told Beau years ago he'd rue the day we took you in. Bad blood, that's what it is. Your ma was nothing but a flirt. I could tell that the minute I laid eyes on her, giving herself all those airs just because she was a Danville. Well, let me tell you about the Danvilles, young lady, and I should know. I married one, and I seen the rest of them. They're lazy no-accounts, that's what they are. Never turned a hand to do a day's work in their lives."

"Now, Mattie," pleaded Cousin Beau. "There's no call to talk that way. It's been a hard day on both of you, and you and Ginny are saying things you don't mean. Why don't you kiss and make up, and then tomorrow, after we've all had a good night's sleep, we'll talk about what we're going to do."

But Cousin Mattie had said too much. Ginny was tense with anger. She might have overlooked criticism of herself, but no one was going to say bad things about Mama. Papa's spunk, which Cousin Mattie had tried to suppress all those years, finally rose to the surface.

Without a word she slid one of the straight chairs across the room. By using it as a step, she was able to reach Stephen Mayhew's rifle, which hung safely out of reach above the door.

"This gun is loaded. Mr. Mayhew keeps it that way." She pointed the muzzle in the direction of Cousin Mat-tie. "Get out of my house. All of you. Right now. And I never want to see you again."

"Well, I never!" declared Cousin Mattie. "Beau—"

"Come on, Mattie," said Cousin Beau, after a minute that seemed to go on and on. "Boys. We're going home."

Ginny followed them outside, still carrying the rifle. She watched them drive away until they turned the bend out of sight. Then she went back in the house and hung the rifle back in place. Finally she sat down in the rocker before the ashes of the dead fire.

How long she sat there, she didn't know. Her anger changed to fright and she found that she was shaking. What had she done? She had actually threatened, at gun point, the only relatives she had in this part of the world. Now she was all alone, and for the first time in her life there was no one to tell her what to do.

The sensible thing was to sell the property and go back to Carolina. She had cousins there, even an aunt and uncle. But would they want her? She had changed during those five years in Oregon. Perhaps she had forgotten all those niceties that went into the making of a lady. Now all she knew was work, how to scrub and clean and cook. Such qualities would hardly be admired back there.

She thought about throwing herself on the mercy of Aunt Lizzie, who seemed to thrive on solving other people's problems. But although Aunt Lizzie and the townspeople would hold no deep regard for Cousin Mattie, what would they think of a person who had actually threatened someone with a gun? And if Cousin Beau hadn't got his family out of there, Ginny might have used it. She had been angry enough. Aunt Lizzie might think the intention was almost as bad as the deed. No, she couldn't admit that.

She wished she had never been born. In the whole

territory of Oregon was there another girl as miserable and unhappy as she? Suddenly she realized that there was. Clutching her shawl about her, she raced outside through the gathering twilight. The next moment she was pounding on the door of Stephen Mayhew's cabin.

"Nona," she called. "Open the door. Bring your baby and come into the house. It's perfectly safe. I'm all alone."

chapter seven

Waste wood," said Nona disapprovingly. "Heat go up chimney."

"A small fire won't warm the room," Ginny told her patiently. The dispute about the size of the fire went on every day. "We can't sit hovered over the fireplace."

It had been four days since she had ordered the Danvilles out of her house and invited Nona in. They had not been happy ones. Nona was not able to give her the companionship Ginny wanted. The Indian woman had no small talk, nor did she respond to any but the most necessary questions. She went silently about the chores Ginny asked her to perform, but otherwise she sat quietly, staring into space. Even the baby, who gurgled on the blanket near the fire, had more to say than his mother.

Nona was not unwilling to do her share of the work. She chopped wood and carried it inside, kept the water bucket filled, milked the cow and saw to the livestock. But Ginny soon discovered that she was untrained in housework and did not care to learn. The dishes that she washed were never rinsed, nor were the clothes. She saw no use in using the heavy flat iron, which was heated on the stove, or in sweeping the floor, and her cooking was of the most primitive kind. Vegetables were baked in the fireplace coals or dropped into a stew, sometimes with their peelings intact.

There was also the problem of keeping her presence a secret. Jim Driscoll had stopped by once to see how Ginny was getting along and whether she needed anything. Nona had hidden in the bedroom, and Ginny was on pins and needles lest the baby cry and give them away. She was sure that Mr. Driscoll would not approve of her harboring his former wife.

In spite of all her drawbacks, Ginny was glad that Nona was there. She wouldn't want to stay alone in a house miles from her nearest neighbor. There were probably wild animals in the forest beyond the clearing. And no matter what Aunt Lizzie said, there might be Indians, too. At least, if an Indian came to the door, Nona could talk to him in his own language and tell him to go away.

"I think I'll drive into town today," she said. "I've got to return all those plates and bowls that people sent their food on. And I want to buy a butter churn and maybe a dress length. I should give Mrs. Heacock back her dress and get one of my own."

Nona did not reply, but Ginny had not expected her to.

"And my toe is wearing through the side of my shoe," she continued, thinking that it was like talking to herself.

The Indian woman looked over from her study of the fire and regarded the shoe that Ginny showed her. It was cracked, and the stocking was plainly visible on one side.

"Nona make moccasins," she offered. "You take gun. Kill deer."

"Moccasins would be nice." Ginny smiled appreciatively. Nona was proving unusually talkative today. That made two remarks in the past ten minutes. "But I couldn't kill a deer. They're too pretty to kill."

Nona did not attempt to hide the scorn in her eyes, but the next moment she turned back to the fire.

Ginny began gathering up the dishes that belonged to the ladies in town. Most of them still held food, but as she had thought, the cakes were dried and the pie crust had become soggy. She scraped everything ruthlessly into a pan for the chickens and poured hot water into the dishpan.

As she washed and wiped, she wondered what her reception would be. Would Aunt Lizzie receive her with her former kindliness or would she accept the stack of dishes and shut the door? From the little she had seen of him, she was sure that Henry Gates would sell her dress goods and shoes. Julia's husband did not look the sort to turn away a customer with money, and Ginny had that.

She had given Aunt Lizzie one of the gold pieces to pay the funeral expenses, but she still had nine of them. A person with money could buy her way into a lot of places, but she couldn't buy friends.

Nona did not say good-bye when she left. She did not even glance up, and Ginny felt a surge of resentment.

"Ungrateful girl," she told herself, then realized that she was speaking aloud. That was Nona's fault, too. Ginny talked aloud to her all the time, and it was becoming a habit. People would think she was odd if they heard her. Only those who were touched in the head talked to themselves.

The beginning of the forest was about half a mile from the house, and Ginny pulled on the reins to stop the horses as she reached there. Yes, the tree tops were whispering today, but it was such a gentle sound she had to strain her ears to hear it.

"Good morning, trees," she said. "Guard my farm till I get back, won't you?"

Even before she drove into town, Ginny began to have doubts about coming. The people who had been so nice would probably turn on her today. Not that she could blame them. It was a temptation to turn the horse and go back home, but she made herself go on. There were the dishes to take back. Plates and bowls were valuable commodities out here. To keep them would be an even greater breach of manners.

She wished now she had asked Jeth Manning what the townspeople were saying about her. Jeth had driven her buggy home, with his own horse tied on behind, the day after the funeral. She hadn't asked him in. The humiliation of Cousin Mattie's behavior had been too fresh in her mind. She could do no more than mumble thank you and watch him ride away. Now she knew it had been a mistake. She should have talked to him about it. One person was easier to face than a whole town, and it would help to be prepared.

When she halted at Aunt Lizzie's door, she could see a curtain move at one of the windows. It was too late to go back now. She got out and tied the horse to the fence, but even before she could reach for the dishes on the seat the front door was thrown open.

"Why, Ginny," called Aunt Lizzie. "Come in. I been expecting you."

"Expecting me?" How could she have known? Ginny hadn't decided until late this morning that she was coming.

"Oh, maybe not today. But soon," Aunt Lizzie told her smugly, teetering down the path on her tiny feet. "I knowed you'd have to bring back folkses' plates and things. 'Course I was some afeared you wouldn't come alone."

"Oh, yes," said Ginny brightly. "I came alone."

"That's good," Aunt Lizzie said, taking a share of the plates to carry. "I probably shouldn't say so, but I didn't cotton much to your cousin."

"I'm so ashamed," said Ginny. "What people must think of me!"

"They're sorry for you. Everybody is," said Aunt Lizzie promptly. "We can't none of us pick our relations, much as we'd like to. I suppose they all moved in on you?"

"No, not quite." Ginny hesitated, wondering how much she dared divulge. "They've got their own place at Dixie, you know. They couldn't just leave that."

"I suppose not. So they kind of divided up. Part of them went back and some stayed on," Aunt Lizzie decided instantly. "Well, I hope it was him that stayed. Looked to me like he needed a good rest, that poor man did."

"No, Cousin Beau went back," admitted Ginny. "They—"

"And left you saddled with her! Oh, you poor child. 'Course you couldn't stay by yourself. That wouldn't do for one minute. And you couldn't leave the farm alone neither, what with the stock and all. Word get out and somebody'd strip the place. Oh, there's folks like that, even out here. Most people's good, but there's always a rotten apple to spoil the barrel. Not all of them Injuns neither, though them's the worst."

Ginny had opened her mouth to stay that Cousin Mattie, too, had returned to Dixie, but Aunt Lizzie left her no opening. As they reached the kitchen, she tried again.

"Aunt Lizzie, I'm trying to tell you about Cousin Mattie."

"You don't need to tell me a thing," she interrupted firmly. "I had my own ideas about that woman ever and afore I laid eyes on her. Sending you off to your new husband with just one dress to your name! I wasn't a mite surprised the way she acted after the burying. Not one mite. They manage to eat all that food, did they?"

"No. There was lots left, but it had dried up or spoiled. I washed the plates."

"Quite right," Aunt Lizzie said. "And smart, too. Because them that had something left might take offense, thinking you didn't like it. While them with empty dishes would gloat. Take off your shawl and bonnet and set. I'll make us a nice cup of mint tea."

Ginny made one more attempt to explain.

"Aunt Lizzie, I don't think you understand about Cousin Mattie. She—"

"Oh, I understand. All too well, so let's not say no more about her. I don't want to hear her name around here again."

"Aunt Lizzie, do you know of somebody, maybe a widow, who is all alone and would like to live with me?" Ginny decided to approach the problem from a different angle.

"No, I don't," declared Aunt Lizzie instantly. "And I've racked my brains trying to come up with somebody ever since I laid eyes on you-know-who. All the decent white women in these parts are married or about to be."

"Maybe there might be an Indian. Somebody the Methodist Mission knows about," suggested Ginny craftily.

Aunt Lizzie looked scandalized at the suggestion.

"The talk it would stir up you wouldn't believe."

"But why?"

"Folks around here don't cotton to Injuns," explained Aunt Lizzie kindly. "You may not remember much about crossing the Plains, but I do. Why, the murdering and scalping that went on just because decent folks was crossing through land that they claimed was theirs, you wouldn't believe. And stealing, too! Why, they was always riding up and demanding food. And you had to give it to them, no matter how little you had."

Ginny tried to think, but that part of the trip was blanked from her mind.

"But they say the Indians around here are different. They're peaceful," she suggested weakly.

"So far," agreed Aunt Lizzie darkly. "But they're still Injuns. You can't tell when they might take it in their heads to go on the warpath. You couldn't make a servant out of a Injun, Ginny, not like you did with the coloreds back where you come from. It ain't in their nature. And if you was to take one in your house, why the folks in this town would think there was something wrong with you. They'd call you a Injun-lover, and they wouldn't have nothing to do with you. Just look at Jeb Hooker. He walks pigeon-toed, and he says he can't help it, but even so, folks whisper that he's likely got Injun blood somewheres back, because that's the way the savages walk, with their feet turned in. Maybe he has and maybe he hasn't, but if he does something crazy one day, we'll know for sure. You don't want folks holding something like that against you, do you?"

"No, no," Ginny agreed quickly. So far the townspeople had been friendly. She didn't want to do anything to jeopardize that. "But what am I going to do?" she added piteously.

"Near as I can see you'll have to put up with you-know-who a mite longer," Aunt Lizzie told her sympathetically. "But I'll ask around. There's nobody here in town, but I'll talk to Doc Boyle. Maybe there's somebody out in the country that I don't know about.

Leastwise, you got your farm. You-know-who can't get her hands on that less'n you let her. And see that you don't."

"Oh, I won't," promised Ginny thankfully. It was some relief to hear that the land was really hers, but she was disturbed at the deception she was playing on Aunt Lizzie. Well, perhaps Dr. Boyle would know of a substitute for Nona and the whole thing could be put to rights.

Aunt Lizzie poured boiling water on a handful of dried mint leaves and set out two cups and saucers. She smiled at Ginny and it made her feel even more guilty. She didn't want to deceive Aunt Lizzie, but she didn't want to lose her affection either. It would be better to think of something else for a while and save this problem for later when she was alone.

"I wanted to buy a few things while I was in town." She added another spoonful of sugar to her tea when she saw that her hostess had taken two. "A butter churn, because Mr. Mayhew doesn't have one and all that cream is going to waste, and some shoes and a dress length. I know how to sew, so I can make it myself. I don't like to go on wearing Mrs. Heacock's dress."

"Of course not," Aunt Lizzie replied. "You'll need more than one dress. One for everyday and one for best. So long as the good weather holds, you'll be coming in for church, won't you? I sort of looked for you on Sunday, but I understood when you didn't come, it being so soon after Stephen's passing and all. Young Pastor Gilbert done the preaching and he wasn't too bad. His sermon was real inspirational."

Pastor Gilbert! In the stress of all that had happened

Ginny had almost forgotten him. But the memories came rushing back, the graceful way he brushed his dark hair from his white forehead, the warmth of his soft hand, the sympathy in his hazel eyes, and that deep, throbbing voice!

"Oh, yes," she said quickly. "I mean to come as often as I can."

"I'm glad to hear it," Aunt Lizzie approved. "We'll drink up our tea, then me and you'll go shopping."

Henry Gates's store carried everything on Ginny's list and he was most eager to serve them. There was a pair of black leather shoes that laced up the front in her size, and while Aunt Lizzie claimed that two dollars was highway robbery, Ginny bought them. After all, there was no choice.

"Got a pair of nice slippers your size, too, Widow Mayhew," Mr. Gates tempted her. "Be mighty thankful to your feet come evening. Soft as a pair of Injun moccasins."

"Injun moccasins! Henry Gates, I'm surprised at you," said Aunt Lizzie sharply. "The idea of comparing shoes made by decent men to trappings made by savages! Don't you know some old squaw chewed up that leather to make it soft that way? If that's the kind of thing you admire, well, all I can say is I don't think much of your taste."

Mr. Gates did not reply, but the color mounted in his face at the rebuke. Ginny hastily declined the slippers. They would be nice, but she mustn't spend all her money at one time.

"We'll look at black dress lengths, if you please," said

86

Aunt Lizzie snippily. It would take some time before Henry Gates would be forgiven for suggesting Indian moccasins were comfortable.

On the subject of Indians, Aunt Lizzie had a closed mind. Ginny could tell there was no point in arguing with her.

There were two bolts of black cotton, one of plain calico, the other of a heavier twill that would do for Sundays, and Ginny took six yards of each. On the shelf were other bolts of gayer material that she looked at longingly, and seeing her eyes, Mr. Gates promptly whipped a couple down to the counter.

"No sense in looking at those," said Aunt Lizzie. "A widow wears black for a solid year."

"Unless she marries again," whispered Ginny. "Your husband said I should be thinking about it."

"That Josiah!" Aunt Lizzie frowned darkly. "What a time to bring that up. Men don't know nothing about what's fitting."

"These just came in," said Mr. Gates. "They'll all be gone soon, and I might not get anything like this green one again. The ivy design is real special."

"I could put it away and save it. And maybe that blue flowered one, too," coaxed Ginny. She was sure Nona would like the blue, and the Indian woman had only the gray calico she was wearing.

"You'll never see the likes of these again." Mr. Gates began unwinding the bolts so they could see the fabric better.

"I'd better buy them when I can," decided Ginny, avoiding Aunt Lizzie's reproachful eyes. "I can put them away. As Mr. Gates says, I might not find what I want next year."

Aunt Lizzie watched silently as Mr. Gates measured off six yards of each. Then he found thread and a pair of scissors, which Stephen Mayhew had neglected to stock in his house. In the process of selecting just the right pair of scissors, Aunt Lizzie lost some of her disapproval, and when Ginny relied entirely on her judgment in the choice of a butter churn, the rest of it disappeared. The bill for everything took most of another of the gold pieces.

"Thank you, ladies," said Mr. Gates, as he loaded their purchases into the buggy. "You got time to stop by and call on Julia, Widow Mayhew? She'd be right pleased to see you."

"No, she don't," Aunt Lizzie told him. "She got a late start this morning. She's got to start home right now. Dark comes early this time of year, and she needs to get there afore it sets in."

Ginny agreed. She wouldn't want to drive home in the dark, particularly through the forest corridor. She dropped Aunt Lizzie off at her front door with the promise that she would start on the Sunday dress immediately.

There was no light burning in the house when she reached home, but that was not surprising. Nona often sat in the dark, content with only firelight. Probably, as soon as Ginny had driven off, she had let the fire die down, applying only a stick at a time. Nona had her own ways and she wasn't going to change for anyone, Ginny thought ruefully, as she headed for the barn. She hoped the Indian woman would like the blue-flowered dress material.

As she stabled the horse, she observed that no hay had been thrown down. The chickens had set up such a commotion as she passed that she knew they hadn't been fed that day. The cow hadn't been milked, either. She could tell because the bag hung full and heavy.

That Nona, she thought angrily, as she started for the house. Turn my back, and she forgets everything she's supposed to do.

The fire had burned down to the single back log when Ginny burst into the kitchen, but Nona was not sitting in front of it. Ginny hurried to throw on a pitchy stick, and when it caught, she added more wood so it would blaze into a real fire. A white man's fire, not an Indian's. She lighted candles with the twisted paper spills that were kept on the mantle, and only then did she begin calling.

"Nona! Where are you, Nona?"

Nona was not in the bedroom, and there was no place else for her to hide.

Ginny raced to the back door and called again. There was no answer from the yard. Nona was gone. So were the baby and the blanket, usually spread beside the fire. And so was Stephen Mayhew's rifle!

chapter eight

*A*unt Lizzie was right, Ginny thought angrily as she went about doing Nona's usual chores. You couldn't trust an Indian! She had started with the milking, but now she realized she should have fed the chickens first. By the time she was finished here, the chickens would have gone to roost for the night. The scrapings from the ladies' dishes were still sitting on the kitchen table where she had left them, and doubtless they had been given no feed. Next she had to throw down hay for the horses, then there was wood to chop and carry in. She hadn't realized how much Nona had taken from her shoulders.

To her surprise, there was an untidy pile of wood already chopped. She carried it inside, stumbling in the darkness, and stacked it neatly by the fireplace. The house was unusually quiet. Even though Nona and her baby added little to the conversation, at least they had been company.

She slid the heavy bars across both the outer doors and wished that she had thought to buy curtain material in town. The windows, with their small glass panes, seemed to let the night inside. Anyone walking by could look in at her. It was useless to remind herself there was no one to look in. The black squares were a menace.

A log rolled from the fire with a bang that made her jump. As she straightened up from putting it back, she had the impression of a face peering in through a window. That was ridiculous. It was just her imagination. There was no one out there. How could there be? But there must have been, for now she could hear noises on the porch. Someone was trying to open the door!

She picked up the iron poker by the fireplace and cowered against the wall. If only Nona hadn't taken the gun!

"Open door!" The voice was muffled, but it was unmistakable.

Ginny's fear dissolved in anger. This was too much, she told herself. First the woman steals my gun and runs away. Then she comes back in the dead of night and scares me half to death. She crossed the room, lifted the bar and swung back the door.

Nona entered, dragging something behind her. The gun was stuck under her arm and her other hand clutched a huge slab of raw, red meat. She was bent almost double under the unwieldiness of her load, and the cradle board on her back was nearly horizontal so the baby stared up at the ceiling.

As soon as she was inside, Nona loosened her grasp on the thing she was dragging. It left a red smear on the clean floor behind her. She placed the meat on the table and straightened up with a grunt that could only mean relief. Then she handed Ginny the gun.

"Nona kill deer," she announced with satisfaction. "Make moccasins." She kicked at the object on the floor, which Ginny could now see was the skin of the deer. "Eat meat. Better than cow."

"You went out and killed a deer?" Ginny gasped. "Where did you go? In the forest?"

Nona shook her head.

"Bad spirits there. Nona wait at edge. Deer come out to eat when sun go down."

Ginny was too glad to see her to stay angry. Besides, Nona had only been trying to do something for her. She had seen that Ginny needed shoes, and she was preparing to make some.

"You gave me an awful fright," she admitted. "When I came home and found you gone, I thought you'd gone away for good."

Nona shrugged. It was an expressive gesture. She had no where else to go.

"You had to waste a lot of meat," said Ginny regretfully. "But I don't know how you carried as much as you did."

"No waste," Nona told her. "Brother Coyote find."

Ginny spent the next day sewing on her new Sunday

92

dress. She wished that it could have been one with the green ivy design, but that would have been unacceptable. A widow had to wear black whether it was becoming or not.

Nona had only nodded when Ginny explained that the blue-flowered print was for her. But she must have been pleased for she felt the material several times as it lay folded on top of the bureau, and she even unwrapped it to study the pattern more thoroughly.

Ginny sewed as long as there was daylight, but at sundown she had to lay her work aside. Her eyes were tired, and black was hard to see by candlelight. Making the dresses was not going to be easy. All the seams had to be done by hand with tiny little stitches that would hold.

The next morning she started in again. She was trimming the bodice with rows of tiny tucks and had decided to add a collar. Of course, it would have been better if the collar could be white, but even a black collar was better than the plain, unflattering neckline of Maria Heacock's mourning dress.

Nona was on her knees before the fire, turning some strips of deer meat, which she had insisted on drying for winter. She had rigged up a little frame on the hearth, made of cut saplings anchored between two logs, and the venison was suspended from that. Every little while she turned it carefully so the heat would reach it more evenly. Now she straightened up, her head tilted the way it always was when she was listening.

"Horse come," she announced, and snatching up her baby with its blanket, she disappeared behind the bedroom door.

93

Ginny stuck her needle in the seam and went to the window. She had heard nothing, and at first there was nothing to see. But she knew that Nona's ears were sharper than her own, so she waited. It was probably Jim Driscoll on his way into town. The Indian woman was right in hiding. He might stop to see if Ginny needed anything.

But the rider wasn't Driscoll. He was coming from the opposite direction, and as he drew nearer, she could see that it was Jeth Manning. For a moment she wished she had put on Maria Heacock's black dress this morning. She had worn her old muslin one because black material on a black lap was harder to see. Then she decided it didn't matter. Jeth wouldn't notice what she was wearing. He was too shy.

But Jeth wasn't shy today. He came right in when he was invited and handed her a basket covered with a white towel.

"Aunt Lizzie baked this morning," he told her. "And she put in some honey, too. Uncle Josiah and me cut down a bee tree last summer."

"That's nice of her," Ginny said graciously. "Won't you sit down?"

"I'd rather look around. This is the first chance I've had to see Stephen's place. Though I seen the stove before. Everybody did. He ordered it through Henry Gates, and I reckon everybody in town came in to look when it arrived."

"That's good," said Ginny. She planted herself firmly in front of the bedroom door. "You probably saw the bed and bureau, too. I couldn't show them to you today because my cousin's lying down."

94

"Not ailing, I hope?" he asked politely.

"Sick headache. She gets them sometimes," Ginny lied. She was sure Cousin Mattie had never suffered from a headache in her life, but it was all she could think of on a moment's notice.

"Drying jerky?" Jeth lowered his voice in consideration for the suffering woman in the bedroom. "How'd you learn how to do that?" He leaned down to inspect Nona's framework of saplings.

"I can't remember. I guess I've known a long time," she said vaguely, hoping he wouldn't press for more details. To her relief he didn't.

"Aunt Lizzie said I was to split you up some wood, and so long as I'm here, I'd kind of like to look around at your farm," he told her. "Everybody says Stephen was a fine farmer. One of the best."

"I'm sure he was," she agreed. "I don't know much about farming myself, but he certainly did everything he could to make things nice for me. Do you want me to go with you?"

"If you want to." Jeth spoke so indifferently that Ginny almost withdrew her offer. That was no way for a gentleman to treat a lady. But then Jeth was no gentleman. He was just a boy, a couple of years older than herself, and everybody knew that girls matured much faster. Still he was someone to talk with, and after Nona's long silence anyone's voice would be a change.

"You go ahead," she suggested. "I'll get a shawl and be along."

Nona was sitting on the bedroom floor in a corner, her baby beside her, when Ginny burst in.

"Stay where you are," she advised. "He's going to

split some wood, but I'll see that he doesn't stay too long."

Nona looked at her without speaking, and Ginny snatched her shawl from a bureau drawer and slammed the door behind her.

Jeth was investigating the root cellar when she caught up with him. It was a fine cellar, he told her. He'd never seen a better. The barn met with his approval, too, as did the cow, the two horses, and the flock of chickens. He felt the handles of the plow and announced that the one his father had owned was more to his taste.

"I'll find one like Pa's when I get my farm," he said, almost as though he were talking to himself. "Not that this might not have suited Stephen better. A man's plow's got to fit his hands."

"You're going to have a farm?" asked Ginny in surprise. "I thought you were going in business with your uncle."

"That's what they want, but it's not for me." His voice was troubled. "Sit inside a room all day? No siree! A farm's what I always wanted. Pa took out a claim when we first got here, but he died before he could prove up on it. My mother died too, so I went to live with Aunt Lizzie."

"What happened to your father's farm?"

"Somebody else has it now. If you don't prove up, build a house, and cultivate a crop and live there, the land goes back to the government. But I'll get me another one, soon as I'm eighteen. A man can still take up a claim around here."

"When will you be eighteen?"

"Next July. But before that I got to figure a way to break it to Aunt Lizzie and Uncle Josiah so it won't hurt them too much. I wouldn't want to hurt them."

"No," Ginny agreed soberly. "You mustn't do that."

"Over that rise must be where Stephen planted his grain." Jeth put the problem away temporarily and returned to his inspection of the farm. "The land's cleared up there to where the timber begins. Want to walk up and see?"

Ginny nodded. She supposed it was her duty to inspect as much as she could of this property, which now belonged to her. To her surprise, Jeth did not start immediately. Instead he stopped, his head tilted the way Nona's was when she was listening.

"Better wait," he advised. "You might be having company."

Were his ears as sharp as Nona's, she wondered. But when she turned, she too could see the light buggy just rounding the bend in the road.

"It's the preacher," Jeth told her grinning. "Both of them. Come to console the widow. Hope you got plenty to fix for dinner. Preachers are always hungry."

Ginny lifted her skirts and started running across the barnyard. She was sure Nona wouldn't answer the door, but what if one of them should peer into the bedroom window? Oh, if she'd only worn Maria Heacock's black dress! What would they think of her, parading around in sprigged muslin with her husband scarcely a week in his grave? Jeth's remark about dinner was upsetting too. Arriving at this hour they would expect to be fed, and while she was as able to prepare a meal as anyone, it left her no time for those little niceties that she would have liked to offer Pastor Gilbert.

She arrived at the front porch just as his nephew was helping Pastor Seaforth from the buggy.

"Pastor Seaforth. Pastor Gilbert." To her annoyance she was breathless and hardly able to speak. "How nice of you to stop by!"

"Good day, Mrs. Mayhew." There was that wonderful, resounding voice, almost like the bass notes of an organ. "Uncle and I are on our way to the Driscolls'. Mrs. Driscoll kindly asked us to take dinner. And since we were passing by, we thought we should look in."

"Widow Mayhew." Pastor Seaforth took her fingers in his fluttery clasp, but his eyes were on her light-colored dress. "You seem to be bearing up in your great loss."

"I try." She looked down in embarrassment. Not only was it the wrong color, but a long, jagged streak of dirt, collected somewhere in the barn, ran down the front of her skirt. "I hope you'll excuse the way I look. I have only one black dress and it had to be washed today."

Since his uncle did not hear all her explanation, Pastor Gilbert repeated it in a louder voice. Ginny stood there miserably, hoping they wouldn't notice the absence of washing on the line.

"To be sure," said Pastor Seaforth, when he finally understood, but his eyes were still reproachful. "It is a sad time for you, Widow Mayhew, and for all of Stephen's friends. We will not forget him easily."

"I wish I could ask you in," shouted Ginny. "But my cousin is sick in bed."

"Sick, did you say?" This time Pastor Seaforth understood. "Your cousin's sick? Then we must go in, Gilbert.

It is our duty to comfort those in sickness as in death."

"What is your cousin's ailment?" asked Pastor Gilbert cautiously.

"Toothache," Ginny told him. "Her jaw's all swollen up, and I don't think she'd want anyone to see her looking like that. It would be too humiliating."

She heard a choking sound behind her and realized too late that Jeth had followed at her heels. He whipped a handkerchief from his pocket and began blowing his nose.

"A toothache can be a painful thing," agreed Pastor Gilbert. "And I can understand fully how a lady might not care to be seen with a disfigured face."

"Come, Gilbert," urged his uncle, after he had greeted Jeth. "We must comfort the sick woman."

"No, Uncle," Pastor Gilbert told him firmly. "It's only a toothache. We are not needed. Besides, we ought to drive on. Mrs. Driscoll is expecting us at noon."

"I hope you'll come back and take dinner with me one day," said Ginny. She was torn between the desire to keep Pastor Gilbert longer and the need to have him away from the house. She wouldn't put it past the older man to knock on the bedroom door to offer his comfort.

"Nothing would give us greater pleasure, dear lady." Pastor Gilbert took her hand in his warm grasp and looked deep into her eyes. Ginny felt her heart skip a beat, and it was hard to look away.

"When your cousin is well enough to receive visitors, be sure that we will be happy to return," he promised. "And I trust that we will see both of you at services next Sunday."

"Oh, I'll be there," she promised. Wild horses couldn't

keep her away. "I can't speak for my cousin. Her health is poor."

Ginny watched as he helped the older man into the buggy and picked up the reins. As they drove away, Pastor Gilbert turned and lifted his hat so she could see his dark hair as it waved gracefully back from his forehead.

"Well!" Jeth's voice sounded unpleasantly loud in her ear. "Let's you and me go inside. I'd kind of like to see what you got hid in that bedroom."

chapter nine

*R*eckon you're Jim Driscoll's squaw," said Jeth thoughtfully, as he looked down at Nona.

There had been no way Ginny could persuade him that it was Cousin Mattie in the bedroom, nor could she keep him from investigating for himself. He was the most stubborn man—boy, she corrected herself angrily—that she had ever laid eyes on. Whatever gave him the idea she was concealing something, she couldn't imagine. True she had slipped when she said that Cousin Mattie had a headache, then changed it to a toothache, but a person could have both, couldn't she? He had just grinned in that lopsided way of his, marched into the house ahead of her, and thrown open the bedroom door before she could stop him.

Nona had been in the same corner as before. She started up in alarm when she heard the door, but as soon as she saw the visitor wasn't Jim Driscoll, she relaxed.

"How long's she been here?" asked Jeth.

"I guess she was here before Mr. Mayhew died, but I don't think he knew about it. I found her hiding in the old cabin. And I asked her into the house myself." The last sentence was defensive, daring him to say something against it.

"Then your cousin hasn't been here at all?"

"Oh, she was here. All of them were," Ginny admitted bitterly. "They planned to move in. They wanted to take everything for themselves. I made them leave."

"How'd you do that?" he asked, puzzled.

"With Mr. Mayhew's gun." He might as well know the whole truth. "I think maybe I might have used it if I'd had to. I was awfully mad at them."

"Just as well you didn't have to." He grinned.

"Nona, get up," ordered Ginny. "He knows all about it. There's no need to sit there any longer."

But Nona continued to sit, her eyes staring into space.

"The jerky's burning," remarked Jeth casually. "I fixed up the fire."

She was off the floor in an instant and through the door. They could hear her mumbling to herself in the next room, something about white men's lies. Ginny picked up the baby and followed.

"I suppose you're going to tell Aunt Lizzie," she said crossly. "And she'll be scandalized. She doesn't like Indians. But I won't have Cousin Mattie here, and there's nobody else. Besides, Nona's a big help. She does all the outside chores, and I—I don't like to stay alone at night."

"There's no need to tell anybody about it if you don't want to," Jeth said reasonably. "If you want to share your house with an Injun, it's nobody else's business. But you'd be smart to make a clean breast of it," he added. "It's bound to come out sooner or later."

"I can't. Aunt Lizzie says everybody'd hold it against me. They wouldn't have anything to do with me. They'd call me an Indian-lover."

"Some of them would," he agreed thoughtfully. "People are funny. They make up their minds about something. Then they get together and talk, and the whole thing gets bigger and bigger. People who weren't even there take sides, and they blame others that didn't have anything to do with it. Aunt Lizzie's one of the worst. Maybe *the* worst, because she won't never let it alone. Her best friend was killed by an arrow on the way out. She can't remember that our people were shooting back and some of the Injuns got it, too."

"But what am I going to do? Aunt Lizzie says there isn't anybody else."

"She ought to know if anybody does," agreed Jeth. "And if you don't want to stay alone, you'll have to keep Nona here. You don't need to worry about me. I'm not going to tell."

She looked at him quickly, wondering how far she could trust him.

"The way I see it, you're safe enough for the winter,"

he continued. "After what happened at the funeral, the town's got no love for your cousin. So long as they think they'd run into her, they'll stay away. That's why Aunt Lizzie sent me today instead of coming herself. Another few weeks and bad weather'll set in. Nobody can get over the road when that happens. You'll be stuck here, both of you, at least four months. Only danger would be Jim Driscoll dropping by. Minute he laid eyes on that contraption for drying jerky, he'd know."

"Is that how you knew?"

"That's how." He nodded, grinning. "No white woman would set up a drying frame that way. And I doubt if she'd make jerky either. That's plain Injun."

Nona paused in turning the strips of venison to glare up at him.

"So that means you've only got to stall folks another few weeks, then you got at least four months to take it easy. Come summer, when the bachelors start courting, you can figure out something else."

"Bachelors? Courting?" She didn't know what he meant.

"By April they'll be knocking at your door," he assured her solemnly. "They'll come from miles around to do things for the rich widow. They'll plow your fields and plant your crops and cut trees till the last cow comes home. 'Course, they won't expect you to say yes right away, but they'll want to get their licks in early."

"Jeth Manning!" She couldn't tell whether he was teasing her, but he looked perfectly serious.

"Just thought I should warn you." He leaned over and tickled the baby under its chin. "Nothing so cute as an

104

Injun baby. White ones can't hold a candle to them. Suppose I tackle that woodpile while you see about fixing dinner? Least you can do is feed me."

She could hear the sound of his axe all the time she was preparing the meal. Jeth had given her a lot to think about. He had promised to keep the secret, and she had to trust him. But was he joking about the prospective husbands? Any girl would be flattered by a throng of suitors, and it would be nice to have someone put in the crops, but it wasn't so flattering to know it was because she owned the farm. And she wasn't sure it would be so much fun spending four isolated months with only Nona for company. Perhaps Jeth was right and she should confess everything to Aunt Lizzie and move back to town. There must be enough money to pay her board for the winter. She said as much when she called him in for dinner.

"It's up to you," he told her, heaping stew onto his plate. "I suppose you could sell the cow and board out the horses. And lots of folks would be glad to take the chickens. But that fine bedroom furniture of Stephen's would likely warp in a shut-up house. And what would Nona do?"

"She could stay here."

"She couldn't stay alone. She's afraid of Jim Driscoll, and I don't blame her much. In her place I'd clear out for good."

"She thinks his wife will leave him pretty soon," reported Ginny. "And then he'll take her back."

"No chance." Jeth turned in his chair and spoke to the Indian woman, who had refused to join them at the table, in a tongue Ginny could not understand. Nona answered eagerly and at great length.

"I didn't know you could speak Indian," said Ginny, when the conversation came to an end. "Where did you learn?"

"Pa took up his claim on the Luckiamute," Jeth told her. "He was one of the first ones out there, and there wasn't anyone for me to play with but a couple of little Injun boys who lived in a shanty close by. I picked up jargon from them."

"Didn't your mother and father care that you were playing with Indians?" After the feelings of the townspeople this seemed hard to understand.

"Ma wasn't too pleased," he admitted grinning. "But Pa didn't care. He said I had to have somebody close to my age. He didn't want me to grow up to be a hermit. I don't talk about it in front of Aunt Lizzie, but I've got some good friends who are Injuns."

Ginny looked at him quickly. This time she didn't think he was joking.

"You can't figure Nona out, can you?" he asked curiously. "I was hoping you could. Maybe you never will, and it's not your fault. Understanding people like Nona is something you're either born with or not."

For some reason Ginny felt uncomfortable, as though she had let Jeth down.

"What did you say to her?" she asked.

"I asked her why she didn't go back to her own people. She's got too much pride. They didn't want her to marry a white man in the first place, but she did anyway. Now she doesn't want to admit she made a mistake."

106

Ginny nodded soberly. Pride was something she could understand. Back home everyone had a lot of it. All the young ladies at Miss Spencer's were accepted only after much scrutiny of their family backgrounds. People took pride in their big houses and their possessions. All the Claibourns and the Danvilles had been proud, all but Cousin Beau and look what happened to him. She supposed that Indians had their own standards of pride and that she should respect Nona's.

"I guess we can manage here," she said after a minute.

"Good girl," said Jeth approvingly.

He started back to town as soon as they finished dinner, and Ginny resumed her sewing. First, however, she changed her muslin dress for Maria Heacock's dingy black. Maybe Pastor Gilbert and his uncle would check on Cousin Mattie's toothache on their return to town. It was with both disappointment and relief that she saw their buggy jolt by without stopping.

By working feverishly she managed to finish the black dress by the weekend, and on Sunday she drove into town. Jeth had told her that his aunt had suggested that Ginny stop by and go to church with them, returning for dinner afterwards. She was glad of the invitation. She felt shy and insecure with all those people she had met only once.

"I'm some relieved to see you come alone," said Aunt Lizzie, peering out the front door at the empty buggy tied to the fence. "Not that I wouldn't a kept a civil tongue to that woman in my own house. Jeth says she's ailing."

"I think she's better," Ginny said evasively. "But

Cousin Mattie never cared much for town." At least that part of it was true.

"So I gathered," said Aunt Lizzie. "Or she'd a come along with her husband when he visited the courthouse."

"Cousin Beau went to the courthouse?"

"She didn't tell you about that? I didn't figure she would." Aunt Lizzie nodded smugly. "He come in to see about Stephen's land. Your land. Claimed you was under age and he should have the management of it. Well, Judge Hawkins sent him packing, I can tell you. Damaris Hawkins was the one that sent the apple pie for Stephen's burying. And apples being so hard come by, she was madder than a setting hen run off her nest not to get so much as a bite of it. The judge he told your cousin that the law was clear. The land is yours, since you're the widow, and you've no need to call in somebody to handle your property."

Ginny smiled with relief. She had been afraid the purpose of Cousin Beau's visit was to accuse her of threatening them with a gun.

She had worried needlessly about her reception by the townspeople. They were as friendly as they had been before. Perhaps even more so. In more than one face she detected a different kind of sympathy than that accorded a new widow. Now they were sorry for anyone who had to put up with Cousin Mattie.

To Ginny's disappointment, Pastor Seaforth gave the morning's sermon, but his nephew offered a prayer and lined off the hymns. Although his hazel eyes swept the whole congregation, she felt that they lingered on her. It was reassuring to know that her black dress was crisply new, and that the discreet collar was more flattering than a plain binding.

Julia Gates came up to them after the service and asked Ginny to come home with them for dinner. When she learned that Aunt Lizzie had invited her first, she suggested the following Sunday.

"It'll be even better," she added. "Because Pastor Seaforth and his nephew are taking dinner with us then."

"That's nice," approved Aunt Lizzie. "They're coming to my house today. We're having fried chicken."

"Oh," said Julia in a disappointed tone. "That's what I'd planned to have."

"That's why I told you," said Aunt Lizzie. "Sometimes preachers get fried-chickened to death."

It would have been nice, Ginny told herself as she ate her chicken, if she and Pastor Gilbert had been able to talk alone. There were so many things about him that she wanted to know. Where he had lived before coming here. What he liked and didn't like. Was he going to stay on and help his uncle or move to a church of his own? And, above all, what he thought of her. Not that she would ever ask him that, but if they had been given a chance to talk there might have been some clue.

With Aunt Lizzie around, such discussions were impossible. Although Ginny and Pastor Gilbert sat side by side at the table, their hostess kept the conversation firmly in hand. Ginny glanced across at Jeth, who was sitting opposite, and he gave her a lopsided grin, an especially knowing one. She smiled politely and looked down at her plate, telling herself that next Sunday at Julia's would be different.

But it wasn't different. Before dinner Henry Gates pointed Pastor Gilbert to a chair next to his own and launched into a discussion on politics. Ginny helped Julia put the finishing touches on her dinner of roast beef, and at the table they all listened while Mr. Gates talked about merchandise and prices and how hard it was to get some people to pay their bills. Ginny helped with the dishes, and when they were finished it was time for her to start home. It was a cloudy day and darkness came early.

At parting, Pastor Gilbert held her hand in his warm clasp and trusted he would see her the following Sunday. She had to be content with that.

Nona was waiting when she arrived home. For once she had made an effort to please. The ashes in the fire-place had been cleaned out. The kitchen floor was swept and the dishes were stacked and put away in the cup-boards. She was sitting on the floor beside a freshly filled woodbox, crooning to her baby. And although she didn't actually smile, there was a look of welcome in her eyes.

Ginny stood for a moment, looking down at her. Poor Nona, she thought. She has no place else to go, no one to care about her but me. And no matter what they say, she would never turn on me. I'm going to keep her here as long as she wants to stay. Besides—what else can I do?

chapter ten

 W̲agon come," said Nona early the next morning, and Ginny hurried to the door to look out.

It was a wagon, sure enough, and it had a built-in structure like a small enclosed room on the back. As it approached the door, the driver began ringing a little handbell.

"It's the peddler!" cried Ginny in delight, and hurried outside.

She knew all about the peddler, although never before had she been free to examine all the wondrous contents of his wagon. Twice a year it had stopped before the Danville door, and Cousin Mattie had gone out to make her selection of necessities for the next few months. There was no store in Little Dixie, and the biannual visits of the peddler saved her a trip to Dallas.

Julia Bridges had told Ginny that most families invited the peddler in. Sometimes he even stayed the night at farmhouses, but he was always invited for a meal. Cousin Mattie never did that. Regardless of the hour, she made her selection quickly from the back of the wagon, then sent the driver on to the next farm as soon as the transaction was completed.

Once Ginny had followed behind and had a brief glimpse of the wares inside, pans and kettles hanging from the roof, boxes filled with who knew what delightful items. Then Cousin Mattie had noticed her standing there and had told her to go back and finish the dishes. Ginny had resented that, especially since Orville and Willie had been allowed to stay and listen while their mother haggled over a pair of knitting needles and a new tin bucket to replace an old one that had rusted. Today, she resolved she would make up for all those times when her only glimpse of the wagon was through the kitchen window.

"Morning, young lady," called the peddler, climbing briskly from the seat. "Your ma to home?"

For a moment Ginny stared blankly. Then she realized that he was alluding to her age.

"I'm the lady of the house," she told him primly. "I'm the Widow Mayhew."

"Excuse me, ma'am." He looked at her curiously. "I must be getting old. I'd heard—I mean, I should have remembered. I'm Abe Nichols, and I make this trip by your farm twice a year. Late spring and early fall, weather permitting."

She almost told him that she knew who he was. Peddlers each had their own territory, and she had watched this one from the kitchen window in Dixie twice a year for five years. Then she decided she might as well hold her tongue. Make a fresh start, that was the thing to do.

"My stock's a little low," he told her apologetically, going around to the back of the wagon. "I always save this for the last trip out. Mr. Mayhew and Mr. Driscoll, being bachelors, don't need so much. But now there's a lady on this road, I'll bring more next time."

"I'd like to see what you have," she said eagerly, peering at the crates and boxes as he pushed back the curtain that concealed the interior.

"You ain't got a list?" he asked in surprise. "Most ladies have one on the ready."

"I will next time," she promised. "I wasn't expecting you."

"How about a new pot?" He unhooked a granite utensil swinging from the roof. "This is a real nice one. Give you lots of service."

"No, I don't need anything like that." Her eyes were on the stacked boxes on the floor.

"Needles? Pins? Writing paper? Now here's something you might fancy, and I only got one left." He opened one of the smaller boxes to display a painted teapot. It had pink flowers on the side, and the handle and lid were outlined in gold. Ginny took it from him carefully and stood admiring it.

"If you don't need a teapot yourself, it'd make a handsome Christmas present for a loved one." The peddler tempted her. "Remember, this will be my last trip till late next spring."

Christmas! Ginny had almost forgotten about it. There was no exchange of presents in the Danville household since Cousin Mattie claimed it was a bunch of nonsense cooked up by tradespeople to sell things. Cousin Beau always made sure there was a sack of hard candy for the children, and sometimes there was turkey for dinner. Otherwise, the holiday was much like any other day. But she could remember Christmases before she came to Oregon. They were always gay times, with festoons of greenery draped along the stairways and crystal bowls of punch, a special one for the gentlemen, another for the children, and all the candles in the chandeliers blazing, and presents! Oh, there had been presents for everyone, gaily wrapped and ribbon-tied!

The peddler was right. The teapot would make a nice present for someone, and she knew the very person.

"I'll take it," she decided instantly.

"It might be a little dear," he admitted truthfully. "Four dollars. But that's real gold leaf on the handle, and the roses are painted by hand."

"I said I'd take it." What was four dollars compared with all the things Aunt Lizzie had done for her? "Do you have any tobacco?" Josiah mustn't be forgotten either.

"Chawing or smoking?"

"For a pipe."

"Yes, ma'am," he told her promptly. "I always carry

'baccy on this run. Both Mr. Mayhew and Mr. Driscoll stock up on that, though Driscoll wants the chawing kind."

After that Ginny selected a string of red glass beads for Nona and a rattle for the baby.

The peddler kept opening more and more boxes, many of which were empty since it was his last run. One contained a man's necktie. He was about to close it again when Ginny told him to stop.

It was a beautiful tie, she thought, quite the most handsome one she had ever seen. It was silk and striped in all the colors of the rainbow.

"I don't know why—" the peddler began, then stopped as he saw the admiration on her face. "Now, ain't that a tie, ma'am?" he asked in a different tone. "I bet there's not another like it west of the Rocky Mountains. Just feel the material. Look at all them colors."

Ginny touched the fabric gently. It was soft as a kitten's fur. She could just imagine Pastor Gilbert wearing it. Not in the pulpit, of course. Even she was willing to admit that the tie was a bit too vivid for that, but he could wear it at home. When he flung back his wavy hair with that characteristic flourish, the soft ends of the tie would flutter gently. Of course, she could never give it to him. It would be unseemly for her to give a present to a man, especially such a man as Pastor Gilbert. But she could keep it in a bureau drawer, and when she looked at it occasionally, she would think of him.

"I'll give you a special price on that tie," urged the peddler. The silence had been unusually long as she thought about Pastor Gilbert. "Generally I'd have to ask at least two dollars for a tie like that. But it's the last one I got left and one of a kind. There wasn't another like it in the bunch. I'll let you have it for a dollar."

"I'll take it," she decided. "Now if you'll count up what I owe you, I'll run and fetch the money. I expect you'd like to be on your way to the Driscolls'." She hoped he wouldn't notice that she hadn't asked him to stop for a meal. With Nona in the house she could hardly do that.

"Yes, ma'am." She was relieved when he didn't seem to notice the oversight. "Ought to get there just about noon. Oh, and, ma'am, I'll throw in this copy of the *Spectator*. I always put one in the cart for Mr. Mayhew when I come by, and I put it in today without thinking. Even though he couldn't read it himself, he said a piece of newsprint was a handy thing to have around. It's free to you, ma'am, out of respect for the widow."

Poor Mr. Mayhew, she thought, as she hurried to the house. If things had been different, she could have read the copy of the *Spectator* aloud to him.

It was raining when Ginny left for town the following Sunday, and she began to see what people meant when they talked about the bad roads in winter. The horse had trouble pulling the buggy through some of the sticky mud holes, and she was so late in arriving that Aunt Lizzie and her family had given her up and gone on to church.

For a moment she considered turning around and going home. She had never faced the townspeople by herself. Aunt Lizzie had always been with her. Although she knew some of them by name, they were relative strangers. She wasn't sure that she had the courage to walk into church alone. Then she told herself that she was being silly and drove on.

She tied her horse in the line of buggies at the rail and plodded through the muddy yard to the door. She was really late. The congregation was singing. After a moment's hesitation, she made herself push open the door and step inside.

The pews seemed to be filled, but the usher, a man she recognized by face but not by name, stepped forward.

"This way, Widow Mayhew," he whispered. "Reckon the road's starting to get bad. You're lucky to have made it."

The lady on the aisle seat where he stopped inched her family along and smilingly made room for Ginny in the pew.

"You're a real good churchgoer, Widow Mayhew," she whispered approvingly. "The rain's kept a lot of folks right here in town from turning out today."

Like the usher, the woman's face was familiar although her name was forgotten. Ginny smiled back, shook the rain from her shawl, and hung it over the back of the seat.

There were no hymn books, so Pastor Gilbert recited each line in turn before the congregation sang it. Since it was a well-known hymn, lining it off this way was unnecessary, but Ginny listened appreciatively to every word, admiring the deep timbre of his voice.

"He'll never get as far as his uncle, that one," whispered the lady, under cover of the rustlings as people took their seats at the close of the hymn. "Gives himself too many airs."

It was a dreadful thing to say about so fine a man as

Pastor Gilbert, and at first Ginny almost told her so. But when she looked at the woman's shiny face, turned to her with conspiratorial friendliness, some of her indignation faded. After all, some people were born incapable of appreciating quality. They couldn't help it.

Several pews ahead she could see Aunt Lizzie's blue bonnet and the backs of Josiah and Jeth's heads. Always before Ginny had sat near the front. Now she was close to the rear, surrounded by almost strangers. But whenever she caught their eyes, the people about her smiled with friendly approval of one who had braved the storm for Sunday worship. It made her feel so warm and comfortable that she hardly listened to Pastor Seaforth's lengthy sermon. How good it was to be accepted on her own!

At the close of the service, her seatmate took her in charge, introducing her right and left.

"You remember Widow Mayhew, Mrs. Simpson? Probably you seen her sitting with me in service today. Don't you think it showed real Christian spirit for the Widow Mayhew to drive in for services in all this rain, Mrs. Cosper? Mrs. Kersey, Widow Mayhew here tells me the road's already getting bad out her way. Winter'll be here before we know it."

Then Aunt Lizzie spied them and claimed Ginny from her new friend, who proved to be a Mrs. Tackson.

"I surely didn't figure to see you here today, Ginny. I surely didn't. If we'd only knowed you was coming, we'd have waited."

"She was perfectly all right, Lizzie." Mrs. Tackson objected.

118

"Thank you for letting me sit with you," said Ginny shyly. She wondered if all these friendly faces would still be smiling if they knew about Nona. Then she put the thought away quickly, because she was afraid she knew the answer.

Mrs. Tackson invited her to have dinner with them, but Aunt Lizzie declined before Ginny could say a word.

"Maybe next spring when the weather turns good," she said firmly. "I doubt that you're all set for company, Emily, and I am. My dinner's 'most ready. I got a chicken stewing on the back of the stove, and Ginny's got to eat quick and get started back. It's a long drive, with the roads getting worse by the minute. Probably the last time she'll get in this year."

At first Ginny was a little resentful. Surely she was old enough to make her own decision about where she wanted to eat dinner. But when they reached the house, she changed her mind. Aunt Lizzie was really serious. Never had meal-preparation been so speedy. In no time at all dumplings were steaming in the kettle with the chicken, string beans cooked up with bits of bacon were heating on the stove along with pots of boiling potatoes, greens, and parsnips. A dish of coleslaw was whisked onto the table beside containers of homemade pickles, chow-chow, currant jelly, crusty bread, and fresh-churned butter. Ginny sniffed appreciatively. Nothing smelled as good as Aunt Lizzie's kitchen at dinnertime. She'd like to stay here forever. But no sooner had they finished their wild blackberry pie than Aunt Lizzie was urging her on her way.

"It's a long drive, child, and the more it rains the

longer it will take. I wasn't joshing when I said this would likely be your last trip in. But you mind your *p's* and *q's*. And don't take no sass from you-know-who. We'll see you come next spring."

Ginny had to agree that three miles through sticky mud took longer on the return trip, but by the time she reached the forest corridor, the rain had stopped and a wind was blowing the clouds swiftly north. The southwest sky was completely blue. Perhaps, she thought hopefully, there would be a few more weeks of good weather after all.

When she turned the bend in the road, she could see a horse tied to one of the apple trees in her front yard. It was a horse she recognized with alarm, for it belonged to Jim Driscoll. She hoped that Nona had remembered to drop the bars on the outside doors, but it wasn't likely. New customs were hard for Nona to accept, and she never barred a door unless Ginny told her to. If she heard someone coming, she would do what she had always done, hide.

There was no sign of Jim Driscoll in the yard, but Ginny couldn't believe he would walk into someone's house uninvited. He might open the front door and call, however. And if he saw the rack for drying venison on the hearth . . . She didn't bother to tie her horse. She left it standing, harnessed to the buggy, and raced up the steps.

The kitchen was empty. She could see that the moment she opened the door. On the hearth, beside the small fire of which Nona approved, was the drying rack with the last of the venison strips.

120

The bedroom door, behind which the Indian woman always took refuge, was standing open. Ginny reached it in two long strides. Nona was huddled in the corner, her baby in her arms, and standing over her was an angry-faced Jim Driscoll.

chapter eleven

What are you doing in my house?" demanded Ginny.

"What's *she* doing here?" countered Driscoll. "You figure maybe to shame me by keeping her around. Well, it won't work. They's ways to make her get, even effen she won't do it on her own."

"I asked her to stay," Ginny told him, hoping he wouldn't hear the quaver in her voice. She thought of Mr. Mayhew's gun hanging over the door. The threat had been enough to frighten the Danvilles, but somehow she didn't think it would do the same with Mr. Driscoll. The minute she pulled the chair across the floor he would guess her intentions and take the rifle. "She's my companion."

"Companion?" He mouthed the word as though it were one he had never heard.

"I can't live here alone. And there's nobody else to stay with me," she explained with dignity.

"You got relations down in Dixie. Get one of them. Or somebody from town. I won't have the squaw and her brat hanging around. I'm a married man now, married proper in a church to a white woman. A man's past is behind him, and it don't have to be flaunted like a redskin flaunts a scalp."

"If you stay off my property, you won't have to see her," Ginny told him. "And if anything happens to her, I'll go straight to the law."

"No, you won't. Because then you'd have to say you been keeping her here. And they're folks in town that wouldn't take kindly to that." Then his voice lost some of its sharpness. "I don't aim to do away with her. Time was when Nona served me good. But now she's got to go. She can't stay here and that's the mortal truth."

"Where would she go?"

"Back to her people. The Molallas. That's where she come from. They'd take her. They was a young buck wanted her real bad, but I out-talked him. Effen she starts tomorrow, she can make it afore the weather turns. 'Tain't like she come from the Nez Perce or Shoshone across the mountains. 'Twon't be too far for her to pack moccasins. The Molallas are just a piece above Willamette Falls."

"But she doesn't want to go back," protested Ginny. "She's got her pride."

"And I got mine," he insisted. "You think I want to shame the new Mrs. Driscoll? Nona's got to go."

"What about the baby?" demanded Ginny angrily. "You're his father. You can't deny that."

"I ain't denying nothing. He's mine all right. My own flesh and blood." He paused to look down at the blanket-wrapped bundle in Nona's arms, and it was a full minute before he continued. "Better that he go with his ma. Anyway you look at it, he's a breed. Parts of two races. I can't do nothing for him. Effen he stays with me, he'd have a mighty sorry time of it. Folks would look down on him all his life. But Injuns is different. To them, a man's a man, no matter what his blood. With them he'd have a chance. Might even be a chief some-day."

Ginny didn't know whether to believe him or not.

"What if they don't go?" she asked.

"I told you they was ways," he reminded her. "First off, I'd hightail me into town and spread the word. Townfolks don't cotton much to Injuns, not them that had kin scalped and massacred on the trail. Somebody'd be out here quicker'n a bobcat could jump a rabbit. And effen that ain't enough, they's other ways."

He turned and started from the room, pausing only long enough to look over his shoulder at the Indian woman. "You pack moccasins tomorrow early, hear? No later than first light."

When they heard the front door slam behind him, Nona got to her feet. She walked quietly into the other

124

room and began turning the strips of venison. When she had finished, she crossed the floor and opened the door to stare out into the darkening twilight.

"Big wind come tonight," she said. "Nona take care of horse now."

Ginny didn't bother to answer. What Driscoll had said affirmed Aunt Lizzie's opinion. When the townspeople knew, all those smiles she had encountered this morning would turn to looks of disapproval. And it had been so nice to feel liked.

Well, there was nothing she could do about it. The best thing was to keep busy.

She moved the venison rack farther back on the hearth and built the small fire into one that would provide more heat. Then she skimmed the collected cream from the top of the flat pans in the back porch and emptied it into the churn. She had planned to make butter tomorrow, but she'd do it tonight instead. She had much to think about, and the years spent under Cousin Mattie's charge had taught her it was easier to think out a problem when her hands were busy.

She had no doubt that Aunt Lizzie would come up with a solution after she learned that it wasn't Cousin Mattie who was sharing her house. But Aunt Lizzie would be disappointed that Ginny had deceived her. She might be angry, too, angry enough so that she washed her hands of Ginny and refused to have anything more to do with her. And Pastor Gilbert! What would he think of someone who had deliberately lied and deceived them all? The only one who would understand was Jeth, and he didn't count.

Nona came back carrying a bucket of fresh milk, and Ginny looked at her unhappily. Poor Nona! She was going to have to swallow her pride after all. She'd have to tell her people they had been right in the first place.

"Eat now?" asked Nona, glancing at the big fire disapprovingly. She seemed to have put Driscoll's visit out of her mind. Ginny was surprised that she was able to take the matter so calmly.

"Fix whatever you want," Ginny agreed. "I'm making butter."

It was while they were eating slabs of corn bread smothered in honey that the real wind started. It seemed to come from a distance like a drum growing louder and louder. It grew nearer and soon they could hear cracking sounds like rifle shots as it tore huge limbs from trees.

Ginny ran to the window. It was too dark to see much, but something huge and branchy swept suddenly across the glass. The very house began to shake around them.

"An earthquake!" she cried in alarm.

"Big wind," said Nona. She crossed to the fire, separating the logs so they would burn out more quickly. "Old ones tell of big wind. Nona never see."

"We'd better get outside." Ginny had visions of the walls tumbling in on them. "Get into the open."

"No," said Nona firmly. "Stay here. Safe here."

The wind continued for over an hour. One of the small glass panes in a window broke, scattering fragments across the floor. Any minute it seemed as though the force would lift the roof from above their heads, but Stephen Mayhew had built well and the roof held. The wind blew down the chimney, filling the room with smoke, and the logs, which Nona had separated, blazed high, then faded to charred blackness. It was as though some giant breath had blown them out like small candles. They continued to hear branches cracking from trees, and sometimes there was a thudding sound as a heavy object was blown against the house.

Finally it subsided. There remained only the usual wind that came through the gap in the Coast Range every evening. The house was steady again, and the cracking sounds ceased. There was only an occasional squeaky bang caused by the barn door which must have blown open.

"Will it start again?" asked Ginny fearfully.

"No," said Nona. "Sleep now."

It was hard to sleep with the remembrance of the windstorm. Ginny had never known one like it, and Nona had said only the old men of her tribe could recall such a happening. She was thankful that she had not been here alone, and it increased her determination that the Indian woman should not leave tomorrow.

Obviously Nona had no intention of leaving. As soon as it was daylight, she built up the fire and went to the barn to do her regular chores. She was still there when Jim Driscoll knocked on the front door.

"That was a granddaddy of a blow." He had obviously put his anger behind him, but there was no apology on his face. "You make out all right?"

"Yes." Ginny did not ask him in but stood in the opening, barring the way.

"Blowed the roof clean off my barn," he told her ruefully. "And toppled a few trees. Tore limbs off so many the ground looks like some squaw's made up a fir bed."

"I haven't been outside to see the damage yet." She peered past him, at her own littered front yard. One of the apple trees, of which Stephen had been so proud, had been torn from the ground. It lay on its side, roots extended.

"Nona better stay another day," Driscoll said gruffly. "Ain't likely such a blow'll come up again, but I wouldn't want for you to be alone effen it did. White women's too delicate for such a scare. I'm going down the road a piece to look at the damage that it done."

Ginny nodded and closed the door. Jim Driscoll probably expected her to thank him for giving Nona one more day, but she didn't intend to. He was a horrible man, and she wondered why Nona wanted to go back to him.

They were eating breakfast when he came pounding at the door again.

"Nobody's going to get in or out of here for quite a spell," he announced glumly. "The blow knocked three big trees plumb across the road. They'll have to be cleaned out first. Squaw, you go get you a axe and help me. It'll take a week, with both of us working, to clear the road."

"Nona's not going to help," Ginny told him quickly. As she saw the angry blood rise in his face, she made her voice softer and she hoped more appealing. "She's got to stay with me. You said yourself that white women are delicate. I'm afraid to be left alone."

"Nothing to be feared of. Blow's all over," he assured her. "My woman's back in the cabin by herself. She ain't scared."

"She's older than I am. Braver, too," pleaded Ginny. "Please, Mr. Driscoll. I need Nona to stay with me."

For a moment he glared as though wondering whether or not to believe her. Then he said something under his breath that sounded like "faugh," before turning and stomping off the porch.

For many mornings after that they watched him go past the house, an axe over his shoulder. He returned late in the afternoon, but he never stopped at the door, and they had no idea how the road clearing was coming along.

Long before he could have finished, however, it began to rain once more. It was almost steady in the way it came down. The intervals between were so short and the air so damp that washings could not be hung outside. Ginny rigged up some lines in the back porch, and something was always drying before the fire.

The weather grew colder, too. Sometimes there was sleet or hail mixed with the rain. The winter that Jeth had told her about had begun. Even if Jim Driscoll had finished clearing away the fallen trees, the roads were now impassable. There was nothing to do but wait it out.

In the dragging days that passed, it seemed to her that the skies were always thick with clouds. It rained off and on every day. It had rained just as much in Little Dixie, but she hadn't been so conscious of it there. In the Danville home there were the sounds of voices, even though they were those of Cousin Mattie giving orders, Orville and Willie bickering and teasing, and Cousin Beau making excuses. Nona hardly ever talked and the baby didn't know how. Each day was exactly like the one before, and Ginny lost track of time.

The paisley shawl was no longer warm enough to wear outside on her brief excursions, so she began wrapping up in a blanket, Indian fashion. Maybe I'm turning into an Indian, she told herself. Maybe Nona's wearing off on me.

Then one morning the ground was white with frost and frozen solid. When she went to the root cellar, she walked over the top instead of slipping ankle deep in mud. At least it's a change, Ginny told herself, and to celebrate she recklessly sawed off a roast from the beef carcass. The beef was diminishing rapidly, and they'd have to ration themselves to make it last the winter.

She built a fire in the stove so she could use the oven. Then, because she didn't want to waste the heat, she stirred up a batch of cooky dough. She was just taking out the last pan when there was the sound of feet on the front porch. Nona, who had been hanging over the table, greedily eyeing the rows of brown cookies as they were baked, grunted and ran for the bedroom. She had been too absorbed in the prospect of the forthcoming sweets to notice outside noises.

Ginny wiped flour from her hands and went to the door. Jeth stood there with two big covered baskets, one over each arm.

"Jeth!" It was as though she had suddenly come alive after being in a long, drugged sleep. "How did you get here?"

"Walked. And I near froze in the bargain." He gave her his funny lopsided smile. "Aren't you going to ask me in?"

130

"Oh, come in. Come in." She threw the door open wide and literally pushed him inside. "There's a fire in the stove. Pull the rocker over here and warm up. I didn't think I'd see anybody from town until spring."

"When Aunt Lizzie saw that heavy freeze, she routed me out." He set the baskets on the floor, sniffed appreciatively, and reached for a cooky even before he began taking off his coat. "She figured it would last the day and I could get out and back before the ground thawed. She sent you Christmas."

"Christmas!" Once again she had forgotten. It seemed years since the peddler had stopped by.

"Only ten days to go," he assured her. "Hello, Nona. How you been?"

Nona had recognized his voice and was peeping around the bedroom door. Now she came into the room and said something in her own language to which Jeth replied.

"Ten days until Christmas," repeated Ginny in amazement. She wondered what had happened to November. Swallowed up by the dismal rain and long silences, probably.

"Your cookies are good," approved Jeth. "Looks like you're making out fine around here."

"We're doing all right." Ginny lied, and it didn't seem such a big lie after all. Everything was better now that Jeth was here. "How's everybody in town?"

"Just the same. Uncle Josiah had to have a tooth pulled and he's swelled up like a chipmunk with a walnut in his cheek, but he'll get over it. Here, you better unload these baskets. Some of it's food that you'll need to use up right away."

He sat down in the rocker, took off his shoes, and held his stockinged feet close to the stove while Ginny began going through the baskets. There was a loaf of Aunt Lizzie's fresh bread, a jar of blackberry jam and another of quince, and a muslin-wrapped square that Jeth told her was fruit cake and should be stored in a dry place for Christmas. Then there were several packages wrapped in white paper and tied with red yarn. A large, soft squashy one was labelled "Ginny from Aunt Lizzie, Merry Christmas," a smaller hard one was marked "Merry Christmas to Ginny from Aunt Lizzie and Josiah," and one in-between-size that bore the inscription, "Season's Greetings, Ginny from Jeth." Tucked into the side of the basket was a striped paper sack, tied up with string and unmarked.

"That's c-a-n-d-y." Jeth spelled out the words as she lifted it from the basket. "It's for N-o-n-a. I figured you could put it away for her till Christmas morning."

"Oh, Jeth! Thank you!" Ginny was almost overcome. How glad she was that the peddler had stopped by that day. "And I've got Christmas presents for you, too. You can take them back with you."

"You have?" He grew suddenly embarrassed, but he couldn't hide his pleasure. "You didn't have to get anything for me, Ginny. I didn't expect a present."

She turned quickly and opened the oven, peering in as though she were inspecting the roast. He had mistaken her meaning. She hadn't meant she had a present for him personally. She had presents for Aunt Lizzie and Josiah that he could carry home in the empty baskets. She had completely forgotten about Jeth. Well, there was nothing to do but give him the beautiful striped tie. Pastor Gilbert's tie!

"My things are in the bedroom," she said, straightening up. If her face looked a little red, he would think it came from the heat of the oven. "I'll have to wrap them. Why don't you visit with Nona while I do it? And by then the potatoes and squash should be done."

Nona was not silent when the other person could understand her own language. Ginny could hear them chattering away all the time she wrapped her gifts. She had no white paper or gay red yarn. She had to use the copy of the *Spectator* that the peddler had left and some of the thread she had bought for sewing.

First she wrapped Josiah's tobacco. The tin container made a neat little package. Then she tore off a sheet to save for the necktie and used the rest of the issue for the teapot. Since the peddler had taken away his boxes, the result was knobby and awkward looking, but the inside would make up for that. The teapot was fragile, and she wanted to give it all the protection she could. Then she took the striped tie from the drawer and held it in her hands for several minutes. It was so beautiful, almost as beautiful as Pastor Gilbert himself. Resolutely, she concealed the glorious stripes in the printed newssheet and tied it tightly. It was her own fault. Jeth was a member of the family. She shouldn't have forgotten him.

"I didn't have any cards or proper paper," she said, when she finally came from the bedroom. "So I'll have to tell you which is for who and you'll have to remember."

"It doesn't matter," Jeth told her quickly. "It's the thought that counts."

His words made her feel worse than ever.

Almost as soon as they had finished dinner, he declared that he must start back. The sun was peeping occasionally between clouds, and if it warmed up, he couldn't walk over the top.

"I'd sink to my knees in mud," he assured them.

"Will we see you again before spring?" Ginny asked anxiously.

"Probably not." His cheerful tone made her want to grind her teeth. "But come March or April things will dry up. The main thing I wanted to know was that you're getting along all right. And you are."

"Of course we are." She tried to make her voice convincing.

"Well, then, Merry Christmas."

"Merry Christmas," she repeated, and tried not to think of Jeth wearing Pastor Gilbert's beautiful striped tie.

chapter twelve

*N*ow that she knew the date, Ginny kept track of the days remaining before Christmas. Every morning she dropped a dried bean into a cup she kept on the mantle above the fireplace. Ten days, ten beans. Then she and Nona would celebrate, just like other Christian people in the world were celebrating the birth of the Christ child.

She tried to explain about Jesus to Nona, and Nona listened so attentively that she thought she was being successful. Wouldn't it be strange, she asked herself, if I turned out to be a missionary? If I really converted somebody? She imagined herself leading the Indian woman to Pastor Gilbert and asking for proper baptism. Of course he would object, saying Nona wasn't a Christian, but when he found out that she'd been converted, how proud and amazed he would be.

"But who has done this thing?" he would ask in his beautiful, resonant voice.

When Ginny confessed modestly that she herself had led the heathen soul into the paths of righteousness, Pastor Gilbert's hazel eyes would fill with admiration and approval. He would tell everyone what a wonderful Christian thing this young girl had done. After that who would dare criticize her for taking Nona into her house?

Then one night, as they sat by the fireplace, they heard a thin, piercing howl from the outer darkness. It was a coyote, and Ginny shuddered.

"I hate those things," she said irritably.

"That Brother Coyote," Nona told her reproachfully. "Old Indian God not like you to say that."

"Old Indian God?" repeated Ginny sharply. "There's only one God, Nona. I've told you about Him. Jesus was His son. He came to earth to save all of us."

"You have Jesus-God. Nona have Old Indian God," the woman insisted firmly and would not discuss the matter further.

Regretfully, Ginny discarded her daydream about winning Pastor Gilbert's admiration by her conversion of a heathen. Nona had listened to the story of the birth of Christ because her people liked to hear stories. But she was unwilling to apply it to herself.

One by one the beans dropped into the cup. When a single bean remained, Ginny tried to approach Christmas from a different angle.

"Tomorrow is a special day, Nona," she explained. "A holiday. A celebration. A feast day. With presents and special things to eat."

"Potlatch?" asked Nona dubiously. Then her face lightened. "You make cooky?"

"Better than that," Ginny assured her. "We'll have Aunt Lizzie's fruit cake. We ought to have a turkey, but we'll have that last ham instead. And I'm going to bring in some fir to decorate. I wish I'd made up that dress material so we'd have something special to wear, but it's too late now. You'll just have to wash the one you're wearing."

Nona didn't want to wash her single dress. She grew quite sulky when Ginny finally persuaded her to take it off to be laundered. She sat on the floor before the fireplace, a blanket wrapped around her shoulders, and refused to help with the work. But her dress needed to be washed. Although the dark gray didn't show dirt, Ginny had to soap again and again before the water ran clean.

When the job was finally completed, she hung the dress in front of the fire to dry and began on the other chores. She had to do them by herself, and there was so much to do to get ready for Christmas! Clean the house. Bring in the fir boughs to decorate the mantle. Fetch the ham and vegetables for tomorrow from the root cellar. It made her happy to be confronted with so many tasks. She sang all the Christmas carols she could remember as she worked.

In midafternoon when she returned from her expedition to the root cellar, she found Nona, wearing her long gray dress, standing in the center of the room.

"Is it dry?" Ginny called anxiously. "You shouldn't

have put it on so soon. I was going to iron it for you."

"No," objected the Indian woman flatly. "Bring wood now."

She wrapped her dirty skin robe over the clean, wrinkled dress and went outside. For the first time that day the disapproving scowl was gone from her face. Everything was again as it should be.

Although their Christmas celebration could hardly compare with those Ginny remembered as a small girl, Ginny was just as excited. Anything out of the ordinary made a break from the monotony of the past few weeks. She could hardly go to sleep the night before. She wished she had a Bible, for obviously they couldn't attend church. But a Bible was something Stephen Mayhew had neglected to stock in his new house. She decided to tell the story of the Christ child's birth again. Nona would listen. She always had. She fell asleep thinking how nice it would be if on Christmas she could make the Indian woman understand. It would be a real miracle, and Pastor Gilbert would be even more impressed.

Christmas breakfast was the usual mush, bread, and milk because Ginny had been too busy with her dinner plans to think of it. But right afterwards they had their presents before the fireplace with its mantle concealed by fir boughs.

Nona was pleased with the red beads and began eating Jeth's hard candies from the sack, one right after another. The baby held his rattle for a moment but kept dropping it, so Ginny turned to her own gifts.

The big squashy package was a hand-knitted black

138

wool shawl, a gentle reminder from Aunt Lizzie that the paisley should be put away for as long as Ginny was a widow. The smallest one from Lizzie and Josiah was a New Testament, and Ginny was delighted, for now she could read aloud the Christmas story in St. Luke. She opened Jeth's gift last of all, and she heard Nona's gasp of admiration as the paper fell away. It was a trinket holder, made in the shape of a small dressing table, with a round, upright mirror in the back. The top lifted up to disclose a hollow box that could be used for jewelry, hairpins, or other valuables. The whole thing was decorated with tiny shells interspersed with pearllike beads. They outlined the mirror and were encrusted thickly on the sides and top.

"Oh, how pretty!" cried Ginny. Jeth must have spent a lot of money on such an elaborate gift. Then she remembered that the striped necktie hadn't been cheap, either. It had cost a whole dollar, and that was a special price.

Somehow the day didn't race by the way earlier Christmasses had done. There was dinner to prepare and eat, and St. Luke to read aloud, and then they were back to their old routine, listening to the rain drum on the roof and splash against the windows. They went to bed early that night, and Ginny couldn't help feeling a little let down.

Afterwards they settled back into living as they had done before: housework, caring for the stock, and watching the rain, which saturated the ground and now collected in muddy lakes in every hollow.

They had a week or two of snow, and Ginny was

excited when she first saw it falling from the sky, covering the bleak yard with a soft, white coat. She wrapped herself in Aunt Lizzie's new shawl and persuaded Nona to help her build a snowman. But it wasn't nearly as much fun as she had hoped. Without gloves, her hands soon became stiff, then numb, and they had to return to the house before it was finished. The snow was pretty to look at from the window, but it soaked through her shoes whenever she had to go outside, and slipped down inside the tops, chilling her feet. It clung to the hem of her long skirts even worse than the mud, and they were always damp and clammy against her legs. She was glad when it left.

Mostly the days were overcast, with periods of cold rain and only brief intervals when blue sky peeped through the clouds. They were all the same, and again Ginny lost track of time. After Christmas, she had dutifully dropped beans in the cup in an attempt to keep track. But one day, when she was soaking a pot of them to be cooked up later, Nona thriftily emptied the contents of the cup into the larger container. When that happened, Ginny gave up. What did it matter? Spring couldn't be hurried. It would come when it was ready.

Luckily they had enough food. The root cellar was filled with vegetables, and they still had flour and cornmeal, salt and sugar. One morning, just as they thought their meat had run out, they found a freshly killed deer on the front porch. Although they saw no signs of the donor, they knew it had to be Jim Driscoll. At least he didn't want them to starve.

It was hard to find things to occupy their minds in the

hours between daylight and dark. Ginny made the two print dresses, the ivy design for herself and the blue-flowered one for Nona. The moccasins were finished and Nona began tanning the second deer hide. Ginny watched carefully, but Nona did not chew the leather to make it soft. She only rubbed it in her hands. Ginny wished she could tell Aunt Lizzie, but of course she never could. The baby provided most of their entertainment. He was sitting up now and playing with small objects, like spoons and empty spools strung together. He didn't seem to care for his Christmas rattle. He was a solemn baby and seldom smiled.

Ginny figured it must have been February when she found the pussy willows. She had plowed through the thick barnyard mud to the chicken house, hoping she might find an egg. The chickens had stopped laying, and the nests were thick with molting feathers. No egg rewarded her search, but on the brown spiky stems of a bush growing near the barn were lines of fuzzy gray knobs. She broke off a handful to carry back to the house.

"Spring's coming, Nona," she called joyfully.

The Indian woman shook her head. "Long time."

"But it's stopped raining. The sun's shining. It even smells like spring."

"Long time," repeated Nona stubbornly.

She was right. After a few days of good weather, the sky clouded over and it began to rain again. The small taste of what would come made the monotony even harder to bear. At least the rain was no longer cold. The ice and snow had been erased by warmer winds from the south, and it now fell in the form of daily showers instead of downpours. But it was still wet and there was enough of it to keep the ground soggy and the road a thick trail of sticky mud.

That's why Ginny was so surprised one day to hear heavy footsteps on the porch. She expected to see Jim Driscoll, but when she opened the door there stood Jeth. His heavy boots were coated with mud up to his knees, and it had even splashed higher, for there were streaks of brown running down his cheeks.

chapter thirteen

"Jeth!" She was so glad to see him, to see anyone, that she threw her arms around him and kissed his
cleanest cheek. "How did you get here? Come in."

"Walked." He gave her his lopsided grin. "I better take
off my boots first or I'll track up your clean floor."

"You walked all the way? I can't believe it!"

"It's only three miles," he reminded her. "But it took
me a while. I sunk pretty deep with every step, and it
took some doing to pull my feet out of the mud. You
couldn't get a horse through now, and you won't be able
to use a buggy for longer than that. But Jim Driscoll
made it to town, so I figured if he did, I could, too. He
told us you were all right."

143

"Jim Driscoll's been to town?" she asked fearfully.

"Probably ran out of whiskey. Nothing else would have been important enough to bring him out." Jeth set his muddy boots against the railing and followed her inside the house.

"People talked to him? And he didn't say anything?"

"About what?"

"About Nona. He knows she's here. It was just like you said. He saw the drying rack and guessed. He said he was going to tell everyone."

"He didn't say a word." Jeth assured her thoughtfully. "I'd have heard if he did."

It was a great relief. Whatever his reasons, Driscoll was going to keep her secret a little longer.

"Oh, Jeth," she cried, putting the unpleasant thoughts of Driscoll from her mind. "I'm so glad to see you. Please thank Aunt Lizzie for sending you."

"I'll thank her." He gave her a strange look, then leaned down to inspect the baby. "Hey, look how this fellow's grown. What's he chewing on?"

"A piece of leather. He's cutting a tooth."

"He's a fine boy, Nona." She actually smiled at Jeth's praise.

"Sit down." Ginny invited him happily. "As soon as the water boils, I'll make tea. Unless you'd rather have coffee. We've got a little left. I want you to tell me about everybody—Aunt Lizzie, Josiah, Julia and Mr. Gates, the Pastor Seaforth. Is Pastor Gilbert still there or has he found a church of his own?"

"He's still there. Everybody's doing fine. Nothing new. Town lost a few roofs and outhouses in the blow, but they're put to rights now. When I came through the woods, I could see where you had a few trees down, too. Driscoll's cleared the road, you'll be glad to hear."

"I know. We saw him go by every morning. It took a long time."

"Well, as winters go, it wasn't too bad," he said cheerfully. "And spring's on its way. Farmers on high ground are talking about plowing now the rain's let up. You'll have to think of that, too, Ginny. Wouldn't do to let Stephen's farm run down."

"I suppose so," she agreed. "But I wouldn't even know where to start."

She'd never plowed a field or sowed a crop. She'd never even spaded a garden. Cousin Beau and the boys had done that while she and Cousin Mattie worked inside.

"What about all those men you were talking about?" she asked, and felt her face flush with embarrassment. "The ones you said would be so anxious to help. Or were you joking?"

"I wasn't joking," he assured her, grinning. "They'll be here, but not until they get their own fields in. And you can't wait for that. You've got to get yours tended to pretty quick."

"Then I'll hire somebody." There were more men than women in the territory. Finding a man to work should be easier than locating a proper companion to stay with her. "Do you know of anybody?"

"Well, there's me," he told her. "I could be persuaded."

"But Josiah needs you. You have to help in his shop."

"I think Uncle Josiah would let me off. He'd think I ought to help out if I could."

"Then I'll pay you," she promised. "I've got money. What do you think of a dollar a day?"

It took so long for him to answer that Ginny wondered if she had offered enough.

"And of course, your dinner would be included," she added coaxingly. "I'd expect to cook dinner for you every day. You want to make money, don't you? You'll need money when you take up your own claim."

"That's right. It'll take money to get started," he agreed. "And a dollar a day's a fair wage, especially if you throw in dinner, too."

"Then it's all settled?"

"It's settled." He had grown strangely serious ever since she had offered to pay him for his work. But now the twinkle returned to his eyes and he gave her the familiar lopsided grin. "This will be the first time I ever farmed a place on my own. I used to help Pa, so I know how, but I wasn't too big. It'll be a good thing to practice on your land before I take up my own."

"I guess it will." Ginny agreed uncertainly. She wasn't so sure she wanted someone practicing on her crops. "When do you think you'll get your own land?"

"In July. I'll be eighteen then," he reminded her. "I heard about some good land down the other side of Albany that I thought I'd look at. Unless somebody files on it first."

"Have you told Aunt Lizzie and Josiah yet?"

"Not yet," he admitted. "I still haven't figured a way to do it."

146

Jeth stayed for dinner, a meal of vegetables, milk, and bread, but lacking in meat. All the beef and ham in the root cellar had been eaten long ago, and even Jim Driscoll's deer was gone. Ginny had been surprised to see it go so fast, although a deer wasn't very big when it was skinned out. Nona, who had cut up the carcass, had been lavish with her servings, and Ginny hadn't realized until too late that it was almost gone. Now they were down to Nona's jerky, which could be soaked and boiled with vegetables to add a little flavoring.

Jeth didn't say anything about the absence of meat on the menu, and he left soon after dinner. It was a long walk, and he told them he wouldn't arrive home much before dark.

"But I'll be back," he promised. "Your ground's not dry enough to work, but it will be before long. Up in the hill it's drying fast."

"And remember, I'll pay you," said Ginny quickly. "A dollar a day every day you work."

"Of course." He grinned and started off through the yard, his boots sinking almost ankle deep with every step.

It wasn't until he was out of sight that Ginny remembered she hadn't thanked him for the Christmas gift. But then, he hadn't mentioned the beautiful striped necktie, either.

It was two weeks before he returned, and when he came, he brought a gift of food. It was almost all meat. The gunny sack slung over his back held two loaves of bread, fresh from Aunt Lizzie's baking, but more important were the large roast, the generous slab of bacon, and a whole chicken, which Nona grabbed and began plucking the minute she saw it. More than once she had suggested that they kill one of the flock behind the barn, but Ginny had been firm about refusing. They needed the hens for eggs and she hoped to raise baby chicks in the spring.

"Thought I'd see how your high ground is coming. It hasn't rained all week and there's good drainage," said Jeth. "And I want to check Stephen's seed wheat in the barn. Some farmers have started already."

He did not ask her to accompany him, and for some reason Ginny felt shy about tagging along without an invitation. At noon when she walked up the slope to call him for dinner, Jeth was plowing. He was whistling to himself, his eyes were shining, and he seemed almost irritated at the interruption. He really does like to farm, she thought. Somehow she had only half believed it before.

"Ground's just right up on the hill," he told them between bites of fried chicken and potatoes covered with cream gravy. "I want to get it worked and the seed in as fast as I can. You can expect me back tomorrow."

"Bring more bird," said Nona, reaching for the neck, which was the last piece on the platter.

"You made a dollar," Ginny reminded him. "I guess you'll need more of them though to get started on your own."

"I guess I will," said Jeth.

He returned early the next day and every day after that. They hardly saw him except when he stopped at noon to eat. He might as well stay home, thought Ginny

148

resentfully, for all the company he is. Once she had gone up the hill to watch, but after the first greeting Jeth had continued his work as though she wasn't even there. Well, at least I'm getting my wheat planted, she thought, and that's what I'm paying for.

They were eating dinner one day when Nona announced there was someone coming down the road.

"Jim Driscoll." Ginny guessed, but Jeth stood up to look out the window.

"No." He grinned as he returned to the table. "It's the first of your beaus, Ginny. Nona, you better get in the bedroom. Take your plate with you."

Nona did not argue. She took her filled plate in one hand and snatched up the baby with the other. The door vibrated with her angry kick as she closed it behind her.

Ginny could not remember ever having seen the man who entered at her invitation, but he assured her they had met at Stephen's funeral. He was tall and rangy, with big hands and dirt-rimmed fingernails. He looked to be a few years older than Stephen Mayhew.

"Otis Wheeler's the name," he announced. "I got a claim the other side of town. It's on high ground that dries fast and my early crop's already in. Figured I could spare part of a day to help a poor widow before I start on the bottom land. Didn't figure on you being here, Jeth."

"I've been working here a spell," said Jeth mildly. "Mrs. Mayhew's paying me a dollar a day."

"You shouldn't ought to take advantage like that, Jeth," chided Mr. Wheeler. "Me, I'm happy to help out for nothing."

"Then you can spade the kitchen garden," Jeth

suggested. "That's crying to be done. Or bring in some of those logs that Jim Driscoll cleared down in the timber. Woodshed's going down pretty fast."

"I'll spade." Mr. Wheeler decided quickly. "And maybe the widow'll stand by and tell me how she wants it done."

When Ginny asked him, Mr. Wheeler admitted that he hadn't yet had dinner. He sat down and she brought a clean plate and utensils, watching unhappily as he carved into the pork on the table. Jeth had brought the roast that morning, and she had hoped it would be enough for two days. Now she could see that it wouldn't.

"Heard your relation was staying with you." Mr. Wheeler looked around curiously.

"Cousin Mattie's lying down." Ginny nodded toward the closed bedroom door. "She's not feeling well."

"That's too bad. You ought to make her eat, no matter how bad she feels," he advised. "That's what took my late wife. Just picked at her food, Millie did. Finally wasted away. First time she got a bad cold, it just took her."

"That's very sad," said Ginny, watching as he cut another slice of roast. Maybe the late Mrs. Wheeler was turned against food from watching her husband eat so much.

But later he proved that he knew how to work. The ground turned quickly beneath his spade and the dimensions of the kitchen garden grew before her eyes. Unlike Jeth, Mr. Wheeler liked company while he worked, and he maintained a steady flow of conversation. Ginny learned a lot about him while he kept her standing there. He had a nice piece of land, but it wasn't as good as

Stephen's. And his house was only logs, but he intended to make it larger someday. He was lonely since Millie had been carried away by her weakness. He'd been a good husband to her while she lived. It was too bad they hadn't children, since Mr. Wheeler was fond of them. He especially wanted sons who could take over when he was unable to carry on. And the way he saw it, Jeth Manning had a lot of gall to charge her for his labor. He repeated that several times.

After a while Ginny stopped listening. All he required was an occasional nod of approval. Finally they both agreed that the kitchen garden was large enough, and Mr. Wheeler stopped.

"I'm so obliged to you," said Ginny. "It was kind of you to help me."

"Oh, I'll come again," he promised. "Got some things I got to see to first, but I'll be back. And just remember, I don't charge you for my work, not like some folks I could name. Reckon your cousin's up by now? I ought to pay my respects before I go."

"I'm afraid not," Ginny told him quickly. "She said she was going to stay in bed all day. But I'll certainly tell her how kind you've been."

When he came down from the field, Jeth reported that the wheat was in.

"I'm going to start on the oats tomorrow," he said.

"You're earning your pay, I'll admit that," said Ginny snappishly. She felt cross after spending the afternoon with Mr. Wheeler.

"I aim to give service," said Jeth. "A dollar a day's good wages."

"It certainly is." They had agreed to wait until Jeth

finished before settling up the amount she owed him. She hoped her money would hold out until the work was done. "I hate to ask you, but would you bring more meat when you come tomorrow? Mr. Wheeler finished off the roast."

"That piece of pork cost thirty-five cents," said Jeth reflectively. "I don't figure I should pay for what Otis ate. But you probably got that much work out of him today."

Ginny felt her face grow hot with embarrassment.

"I'll get my purse," she said stiffly.

There was only a nickel and a dime in change left in the bottom, so she had to get one of the gold pieces from the sugar bowl.

"Take it out of that. And for the other meat you bought too. So long as you're about it, you might as well take out your wages so far as you've gone. Let me know when it's used up."

He nodded agreeably.

"I didn't think about your paying for that meat," she apologized. "Though I should have. I expect to pay my way."

The following day another stranger appeared to offer his services to the widow. This was a John Cleaver, a man so elderly that at first Ginny was sure his motives were unselfish. He soon put her straight on that. Mr. Cleaver was tired of living with his son. He thought it was time he remarried and had a place of his own. There was lots of life in him yet, he assured her, and there probably was because he cleaned up all the fallen limbs and debris left from the storm and burned them. There was nothing wrong with his appetite either. Not even a neck remained from the two chickens she had fried.

It was a relief when no one appeared the third day, but on the fourth morning there were two men who arrived separately. Ginny was so flustered she never did get their names straight. All she noticed was that they seemed old. All the men who had come courting her favors had been old. Weren't there any unmarried young men in the territory outside of Pastor Gilbert? The young men she had seen in church all had wives clinging to their arms.

Fortunately, Jeth took charge. He had the men tighten up the barn door, which had sprung loose in the storm, haul manure and spread it for the garden, and clean out the chicken yard. After their enormous noon meal, they were reluctantly persuaded to help him finish the oats.

"I can't get anybody to cut up logs and haul them in for firewood," he told Ginny later. "Unless, of course, you'd be willing to go along and watch them swing an axe."

"No, thank you." She glared at him for even suggesting such a thing.

"Well, it's cheaper than hiring me to get your work done," he pointed out. "All it costs you is their food."

"I doubt if I'd break even on that. And you've forgotten the wear and tear on my ears while I listen to what fine fellows they all are," Ginny reminded him bitterly. "And all those lies I have to tell. Every one of them wants to meet Cousin Mattie."

"You can't blame them for that," Jeth pointed out. "They're courting. Naturally they want to meet your kinfolk."

153

"Courting!" Ginny snorted contemptuously. "Those old men!"

After that, there was a procession of volunteer helpers, some of them, including Mr. Wheeler, who had been there before. They were not too interested in working when they learned that their labors required their being away from the house and Ginny's company, but they always ate big dinners. She began to dread their presence. It was all she could do to be polite.

After the sun came out, the standing puddles dried rapidly, and Jeth reported that the roads were now dry enough for a buggy. Ginny drove in for church the following Sunday.

It was good to see the little town again, and it seemed that she'd been away for a long, long time. Aunt Lizzie greeted her enthusiastically.

"My, I did worry, you being stuck out there with that woman and all. It's a wonder you kept your wits about you. But when Jeth come home and said he'd walked out there and you was doing fine, I felt considerable better."

"You mean you didn't send him that first time?" asked Ginny in surprise. "It was his idea?"

"All his," agreed Aunt Lizzie smiling. "He's my sister's own child. She was always the thoughtful kind, doing for folks and all. That's why Josiah was willing to let Jeth off from the shop when he reminded us how you two poor womenfolk needed help. Though I'm some surprised that nobody else showed up. After all, it's six months since poor Stephen was took."

"There have been a few who stopped to help me," said Ginny slowly. It was clear that Jeth was not reporting everything to Aunt Lizzie. "But no one has worked as hard as Jeth," she added honestly.

Aunt Lizzie beamed and said it was time they started for church.

To Ginny's delight, Pastor Gilbert gave the sermon. This time she was sure that his eyes lingered on her longer than on anyone else. And when he thanked God for bringing everyone present safely through the cold winter, she was positive he was speaking of her.

On the way out, his handclasp was especially warm, almost too warm, for afterwards Ginny had to wipe dampness discreetly on the folds of her shawl.

"Mrs. Mayhew." He dropped his deep voice almost to a whisper. "I hope that by next Sunday I will have something to tell you. Joyful news!"

She wasn't quite sure what he meant by that, and she didn't have time to wonder just then. Jeth, who was right behind, stepped awkwardly on her heel, and Aunt Lizzie turned to see what was keeping her.

She remembered Pastor Gilbert's words on the way home and decided they could mean anything. Maybe he had been given a new church, a fine big church in a town like Oregon City or Salem. Whatever it was, he wanted to share his secret with her. It was very flattering, but it didn't seem nearly as important as it might have before.

When she reached home, she stabled the horse and started for the house. The backyard looked neat and tidy after Mr. Cleaver's efforts, and the vegetable garden, newly planted to peas and carrots, string beans, squash, and turnips, looked fine. Aunt Lizzie had offered Ginny some onion sets, but she had forgotten to pick them up on leaving. She hoped Jeth would bring them when he came tomorrow. Beyond the spaded garden and over a little slope was where they'd decided to put in potatoes. She'd need a lot of those, and there hadn't been room in the patch Mr. Wheeler had spaded. Jeth had promised to plow another section for them. It was funny how much she had come to depend on Jeth, she told herself. But of course, it wasn't like he was doing it for nothing. He was being paid for everything he did.

She let herself in at the back, through the enclosed porch that served as a pantry, and opened the second door. There she stopped, and her heart began to pound furiously.

Standing in the center of the room was a strange man, an Indian. His long black hair hung below the shoulders of his coat and the brown face that stared into hers was hostile. In his hands was a rifle, Stephen's rifle, which was missing from the wall above the door.

chapter fourteen

"Who are you? What do you want?" Although she tried, Ginny could not keep her voice steady. She remembered all those terrible things Indians did to whites—killing, scalping, burning their houses, stealing their livestock. She wanted to get away from there, but her legs wouldn't carry her.

The man did not answer. He stood where he was, his black eyes staring back at her with an expression she could not read.

Then suddenly, from where she had been sitting on the floor before the fire, Nona rose and stepped over to the man. She took the rifle from his hands, crossed the room, and hung it back where it belonged.

157

"This Charley," she said. "Molalla. Want me."

"He wants you?" Ginny didn't know whether to be relieved or even more afraid. "But he can't have you."

The man turned to speak to Nona in that language Ginny could not understand. The speech went on and on, and Nona listened quietly. When he was silent, she interpreted the most important part to Ginny.

"Charley wait long time for Nona."

Why, this must be the rival Driscoll had mentioned, thought Ginny, the tribesman from whom he had stolen Nona. It was a little romantic to think of the man searching all this time and finally discovering his lost love.

"But why did it take him so long to find you?" she asked. "I thought Indians could follow tracks. Read signs along the road."

"Charley in white man jail when Nona go."

"In jail! What for?"

"Drink firewater. Fight." Nona shrugged indifferently.

"Then he's certainly no one for you to go away with." Ginny was horrified. "What if he got drunk again and hurt you?"

Nona did not answer, but she did not look afraid.

"How did he finally find you?" Ginny persisted. "No one knew you were here."

"Jim Driscoll go to Molalla village. Jim Driscoll say."

That Jim Driscoll again, thought Ginny angrily. He must have decided that pressure from the townspeople wouldn't be enough to get rid of his former Indian wife. As soon as the weather cleared, he had ridden to the Molallas for his old rival. But it was still a little romantic

158

to think that Charley's love had remained constant all this time.

"Jim Driscoll give Charley horse," said Nona, shattering Ginny's illusion. "Now Charley stay. Stay till Nona go."

"Stay here? But he can't. I won't have him." She could just imagine what the townspeople would say if they ever heard that she had two Indians living with her. One, and a woman, was bad enough, but even she could understand that harboring an Indian man as well would be unforgivable.

"Sleep in cabin," Nona told her calmly. "Eat here."

Nothing Ginny could say would change her mind.

Nona had already started supper. A stew of vegetables and meat was cooking in the crane above the fireplace. Now she began serving it to Charley, and not until he had finished, would she permit Ginny to ladle out a bowl for herself.

Ginny stood by, watching helplessly as he gulped down the stew. Several times she tried to reason with the Indian woman, but Nona had said all she was prepared to say.

When he had finished his second bowl, Charley left by the back door. He was obviously headed for the cabin.

"We'll talk about this again tomorrow, Nona," Ginny said firmly, but once again she was ignored. So far as Nona was concerned, the matter was closed.

Ginny finally went to bed, her mind filled with disturbing thoughts. Tomorrow, though, Jeth would come and she could lay the problem on his shoulders. Jeth would know what to do. He always did.

But Jeth didn't arrive the next morning. She looked for him until afternoon before she finally gave up. Maybe Josiah had received a special order, more than he could attend to by himself, and Jeth had decided he ought to stay and help his uncle.

She was glad no prospective husbands appeared the next morning. She wouldn't have known how to explain Charley's presence, and he refused to remain out of sight. Since midday he had been sitting on the front steps in plain view, doing absolutely nothing. Ginny had complained to Nona about it, but as usual there was no reply. Today, Nona's generally placid face wore a strange expression. On anyone else it would have been called smugness.

"Horse come," she announced, and Ginny, who had learned to respect Nona's hearing, raced outside. It was late for Jeth, but maybe he had ridden out to explain his absence. She hoped desperately it wouldn't be a suitor.

It proved to be neither. It was Jim Driscoll. He turned in off the road and stopped in front of the steps.

"*Klahowya*, Charley," he said gravely. He did not dismount but sat looking down from his saddle.

"*Klahowya*," answered Charley.

Driscoll began speaking in the Indian's language, and Charley answered in the same tongue. Ginny listened intently, but she couldn't understand a word they were saying. The strangest thing was the change that had come over Charley. No longer was he the dour, suspicious-eyed savage who made little prickles of fear run down Ginny's back every time he looked at her. As he talked with Jim Driscoll, his face lightened, his mouth

160

widened in a smile. Several times he laughed aloud, and once he even bent almost double with mirth. Jim Driscoll laughed too, and if she hadn't known better, Ginny would have sworn the two were exchanging jokes. But such a thing was impossible. Indians didn't tell jokes. Their minds were too full of murderous schemes, at least according to some people.

The talk was interrupted when the front door was thrown open. Something dark was tossed outside and came sliding down the steps. Immediately afterwards the door was slammed shut.

The two men looked at the thing on the steps, then Driscoll began to laugh. He said something to Charley, who nodded, smiling.

"What's happened?" cried Ginny. The object on the steps was easy to identify. It was Nona's old skin robe, the one she always wore when she went outside.

"The squaw's just divorced me," explained Driscoll. "I give her that skin blanket once, and now she's flang it out the door. That means she's shut of me and likely she'll go with Charley here. He's had his eye peeled for her quite a spell."

"Oh," said Ginny weakly. She'd never known anyone who had been divorced, and certainly she didn't think the proceedings were as easy as this. But maybe Indian divorces were different.

Jim Driscoll said something to Charley, who came down the steps holding out his hands. From the pocket of his leather jacket the white man produced a tobacco pouch. He poured its contents into the cupped brown palms. Then he rode away. As Charley transferred the loose tobacco into his own pocket, Ginny saw that he was still smiling.

There was only bacon in the way of meat tonight, for Ginny had depended on Jeth to buy a supply and bring it with him. As usual, Nona served Charley first, and although Ginny pointedly sat at the table, Nona refused her a plate until the man had eaten. He finished all the bacon except for two slices, and for a minute Ginny considered taking them both. But she couldn't do this to the Indian woman, so she took only one.

Nona was acting very unlike herself this evening. Where she had been glum, now she giggled. There was a conquetishness about the way she saw to Charley's comfort, giving him the biggest baked potato, heaping it with butter, running to find a coal to light the pipe he filled with Jim Driscoll's tobacco. For the first time since it was made, she had put on the blue-flowered dress. It was as though she had been saving it for some special occasion and the time had come.

Usually they sat about the fire an hour or two after darkness fell, but tonight Nona banked the fire early, turning the oak log so it would smolder until morning after the fire had burned away. The baby had dropped off to sleep long ago, and now Nona picked him up and tucked the blanket firmly about him. Charley stood up and started for the door, and this time Nona followed.

It took a minute before Ginny realized her intention, then she raced after them.

"Nona! You can't go sleep in the cabin. You're not married to him yet!"

"Marry Charley in Molalla village." Nona paused long

enough to explain. "Charley Nona's man. Jim Driscoll big mistake."

Ginny knew there was no stopping her. She went back to sit before the fire, her head in her hands. Nona was like a child. She didn't know what she was doing, but Ginny knew. Nona was out there in the cabin committing a mortal sin, breaking one of the ten commandments. Some people said Indians didn't have souls, but she knew better. Indians were like other people. Nona had proved that. It was terrible to think how she was endangering her after-life.

If only Jeth had come today, maybe he could have got rid of Charley. But just when she needed him most, Jeth hadn't come. What if he never came again? She didn't know how she could manage without him. He had become part of her life. He was more important than—well, anybody else she knew. Tomorrow if he didn't come, she'd go into town and find him. She'd offer him two dollars a day, since making money was all he cared about. And she'd promise never to argue with him again or to do anything that might displease him. She'd even try to understand Indians.

But what if he wouldn't come? For a short time she toyed with the idea that Jeth might be sick, but Jeth was never sick. He was the healthiest man she'd ever known. An accident though—she put that idea away firmly, refusing to consider it. When he came riding up the road tomorrow, there would be a reasonable explanation for his absence. Of course, it might be Josiah or Aunt Lizzie who had been taken ill. Jeth would have to stay in town and look after them. He wouldn't be free to come here anymore. In that case, Ginny would go to town, too, and nurse them. She'd give them such loving care that Jeth would be forever in her debt.

When the fire burned low, she went to bed. The house was frighteningly still, and she was acutely aware of every noise from without. The wind found a board to bang somewhere. An owl hooted. There was a scratching noise below the window as some animal from the woods made a nighttime inspection of territory it was afraid to explore by day. Ginny had never spent a night alone, and she resolved she'd never do it again. Tomorrow, after Nona left, she'd go back to town with Jeth. Certainly he would come tomorrow.

He wasn't there by breakfast time. Ginny had expected Nona and Charley to leave early, but Nona explained that Jim Driscoll had promised them a bride-price, a blanket. It was for Nona's father, and since it was Nona's second marriage one good blanket would be sufficient.

"Maybe Jim Driscoll's changed his mind," suggested Ginny as the sun mounted higher. "Maybe he's not going to give you a blanket after all."

Nona did not answer, but her head tilted sideways, the way it always did when she was listening.

Ginny listened, too. She heard someone on the road, but he was coming from town, not from Driscoll's claim. It's Jeth, she told herself thankfully, but her spirits fell when a light buggy rounded the turn. Jeth wouldn't be driving a buggy.

As it drew nearer, she could recognize the driver. It was Pastor Gilbert, but a Pastor Gilbert she had never seen. His pale face beneath the straight black hat was set in lines of stern disapproval. The hazel eyes were flashing with indignation. He stopped the horse just before the steps and alighted with angry dignity.

"I have come for an explanation," he said stiffly. "You have deliberately lied to me, Mrs. Mayhew, and have deceived the townspeople as well. You have led us to believe that you were living here, chaperoned by your cousin, while all the time that worthy lady was residing with her husband in their own home. If you were of a suitable age, society might condone your staying by yourself. But you are just a girl. An innocent girl at that. How could you have jeopardized your reputation by such conduct?"

"But I wasn't alone," protested Ginny. "I know I lied about Cousin Mattie, but I wasn't alone. Nona was with me all the time."

"Nona? Who is Nona?"

"Jim Driscoll come now." Nona interrupted in a pleased voice, and Charley grunted his approval.

"You mean you were staying alone with an Indian? Two Indians? Two savages?" exclaimed Pastor Gilbert, once Nona's identity was established. "What have you done to me, Mrs. Mayhew? I am a young minister, just getting started in his calling!"

"I can't see what it's got to do with you, Pastor Gilbert." She began to wonder what she had ever seen in him. The beautiful organlike tones had disappeared in his hysteria.

"Because the story may get out," he told her. "Someone may get wind of it."

"Get wind of what?" Clearly the man was out of his mind.

"Yesterday, Mrs. Mayhew," he said with a small return of his former dignity. "I drove to Little Dixie. I called upon your cousin, Mr. Danville, for his permission to court you. It was the proper thing to do. You can imagine my amazement to find Mrs. Danville there and to hear from her own lips that the whole family had departed after Mr. Mayhew's funeral and that they had not been back."

"Did they tell you why they left?" she asked cautiously.

"They said it was by your own wish. It is their opinion, Mrs. Mayhew, that you have taken leave of your senses, and I'm afraid that I share their views. There was also something said about bad blood in your family—but we will not go into that. Oh, to think of the snare into which I nearly tumbled. The reputation of a pastor's wife, Mrs. Mayhew, must be above reproach. But I was misled by a pretty face, a decorous manner. Surely, it must have been Satan who was tempting me."

He removed his hat to wipe his perspiring forehead and Ginny looked at him critically. At the too pale face, the carefully combed wavy hair that he probably spent hours grooming before a mirror, at the soft hands that had never done an honest day's work in their life. She glanced over to see Jim Driscoll watching them from a distance. He was astride his horse, and there was a striped blanket tied behind the saddle.

"I don't see what you're so worried about, Pastor Gilbert," she said impatiently. "We aren't married. We aren't even engaged to be."

166

"Amen to that," he told her fervently. "But during my call upon your cousin, I'm afraid I expressed myself too fully before I discovered the real circumstances. If he should say something—"

"I don't think you need to worry about anyone finding out about your call on my relatives. Cousin Beau doesn't get into town much, and when I see him, I'll ask him to keep quiet about your intentions," Ginny told him coldly. Then her tone changed, for she had just had an idea, quite the most brilliant idea in her entire life. "And I won't tell either, providing you'll do something for me."

"And what is that, Mrs. Mayhew?"

"I want you to marry these two people." Ginny raised her voice so she could be sure it would carry to Jim Driscoll. She didn't want him to change his mind and try to take Nona back some day. "Their names are Nona and Charley, and they're going to be married anyway as soon as they get home, but I'd like you to do it now."

"Are they Christians?" he asked doubtfully.

"Best possible kind they is," put in Jim Driscoll, riding toward them. "I knowed them both for many a year, Pastor, and I can vouch for them."

"Well, in that case—"

" 'Course Charley don't speak no English," continued Driscoll. "But you get right along with the ceremony. 'Tain't the first time I acted the interpreter."

He swung down from his horse and spoke rapidly to the two Molallas in their own language. What he said Ginny had no idea, but she was relieved when Charley finally nodded his head. At least Nona will be properly married, she told herself. She won't have to live in sin.

167

"I don't believe this is quite—I'm not sure—" Pastor Gilbert hesitated. Plainly he was not certain of the propriety of what he was being asked to do.

"It's going to come out about me, anyway," said Ginny. "About my staying here all winter with Nona. But nobody needs to know about you if I don't tell them."

"Very well." Pastor Gilbert agreed after a moment. He turned to Jim Driscoll. "Please tell the couple to join hands."

Jim Driscoll repeated the instructions, and after some argument, Charley reluctantly took Nona's hand. She had to put down a large bundle wrapped in the last deerhide she had tanned for him to do so. She wore the blue-flowered dress, and the baby, now so large that he protruded from the cradle board, was tied on her back. Charley's free hand clutched the lead rope of the horse Driscoll had given him. They stood patiently because the former trapper told them they must endure this strange whim of the white man.

It was the first wedding Ginny had attended since her own to Stephen Mayhew. Only she and Jim Driscoll seemed happy about it. Charley made his responses at Driscoll's prompting in his own tongue. Nona nodded and said yes when Ginny squeezed her arm. Pastor Gilbert hurried through the ceremoney with a speed his congregation in town would never have recognized.

"I now pronounce you man and wife," he concluded. "You may kiss the bride."

Jim Driscoll shook his head. "That's too much to ask, Pastor. Now they got the blanket, they want to be heading home."

168

Charley had already unfastened the blanket from Driscoll's horse and was preparing to tie it on his own. Nona hesitated a moment before she followed.

"Good-bye, *tillicum*," she said to Ginny. Then she added something in her own tongue before she started after her new husband.

Ginny was disappointed. Jeth had been right. She could never understand Indians. She had taken Nona in when the woman had no place else to go. They had spent six months together. She had even arranged for a proper marriage. Surely there could have been some gratitude expressed, some feeling.

"Nona called you friend," said Jim Driscoll. "That's pretty high praise coming from a Molalla. They don't cotton much to whites. And she asked the Old Indian God to soften your heart so you won't keep your man dangling too long. She says he's a good man. Better take him afore another woman does."

Ginny looked at him blankly. What was Nona talking about? Which of those would-be suitors, whom she could only have glimpsed from the bedroom window, had struck her fancy?

"I trust you will remember your promise, Mrs. Mayhew." Pastor Gilbert lifted the iron weight attached to a rope, with which he had tethered his horse, back into the buggy. "I have kept my part of the bargain. Now you must keep yours."

"I will." She promised quickly. "You can rely on me, Pastor Gilbert. Thank you for the wedding."

He touched his hat automatically and clucked to his horse. His pale face, as he drove away, was distinctly worried.

"Well, now, how about you, Widow?" asked Jim Driscoll when they were alone. "What you calculate to do? Stay on alone?"

"I can't." She shuddered, remembering the noises below her window last night. "I'd go into town only there's the stock to take care of."

"That's nothing to fret about. The pasture grass is greened up. The horses can be turned out. I could stop by every few days and throw down enough grit for the chickens."

She looked at him gratefully. "But there's still the cow. She has to be milked twice a day."

"My woman's been after me to get a cow," he told her. "Effen you don't want to sell yours, maybe I could lead her home on lend."

"Oh, would you?" Maybe she had been wrong about Jim Driscoll being all bad. He was doing his best to be cooperative.

"I s'pose you could tell folks your cousin was called home sudden like. That way you wouldn't have no call to say Nona was here at all," he said.

It was a temptation, but Ginny turned it down.

"No, I'm going to tell the truth. It will come out someday. And if they want to hold a nice girl like Nona against me—well, I can always come back here."

"Reckon you can," agreed Jim Driscoll.

chapter fifteen

I just don't know what come over that boy," repeated Aunt Lizzie. She had been saying the same thing over and over ever since Ginny arrived.

Jeth was gone. He had left early two days before while everyone was still asleep. There was a note saying he was going south, down around Albany, to look for land. He appreciated everything they had done for him, but he just couldn't go into Josiah's business. He'd always wanted to farm, and after working on Ginny's land he was even more convinced that it was what he was meant to do. They'd hear from him as soon as he had established himself, and he was sorry to leave this way, but he couldn't find the words to tell them.

171

"He can't even file on land." Aunt Lizzie shook her head helplessly. "Not lessen he lies. Jeth ain't eighteen yet."

"He wouldn't be the first person to lie. I lied," Ginny reminded her. "And my lie was worse than his."

"It was real wicked of you." Aunt Lizzie agreed. "It wasn't nice what you done, Ginny Mayhew. Not nice at all. And it was a mighty dangerous thing to do, living with a savage that way. You could have woke up dead in your bed one night. But you was just trying to save me stewing about you, which I would have. I wouldn't have slept easy one night knowing about it. It's even worse that Jeth knowed and didn't let on. Where do you figure he is now, Ginny? How far's he got?"

Ginny patted the plump shoulder comfortingly, but she couldn't answer. Aunt Lizzie didn't expect her to. She just needed someone to listen while she thought out loud.

Ginny had made a full confession as soon as she arrived, but Aunt Lizzie was so upset about Jeth that she had not been able to give it her usual attention. Half-heartedly she declared that Ginny had done wrong in deceiving everyone. But after all, the savage hadn't stolen anything and she was gone now. Just as poor Jeth was gone. The thought brought on another flood of tears.

Ginny was concerned about Jeth too. It was unlike him to run away like this. He was always so dependable, so understanding. She had thought she knew him, that he confided in her. But obviously she had been wrong. He hadn't said one thing about going away so soon. It was always "some day."

"How far is Albany?" she asked. "That's where the letter said he was going. Maybe somebody should go after him."

"Near to a hundred miles," wailed Aunt Lizzie. "I never been there myself. We'll never see him, not ever again. It'd take three, maybe four days, to get there."

Ginny gasped. A hundred miles! She had no idea it was so far. Aunt Lizzie was right. It could be years before they saw Jeth again.

"If he was so set on farming, though he never said one word to me and Josiah, why couldn't he have settled close to home? We wouldn't of stood in his way. I always hoped—" Aunt Lizzie broke off with an embarrassed little laugh.

"You hoped what, Aunt Lizzie?"

"Well, I know it's silly, but I'm right fond of you both. So I sort of hoped maybe you and Jeth might make a go of it. Oh, I know he's young, and most girls cotton to older men. One who's already settled. But I think Jeth hoped so, too, him being so sweet on you and all."

"Jeth? Sweet on me?"

"Well, of course he was," said Aunt Lizzie positively. "Why else do you think he done all that work on your land? And walked clear out to see you with the mud up above his knees? I had to wash every stitch of clothes he wore when he got back. And that necktie you give him for Christmas! I just wish you could have seen his eyes when he opened it up. I never could get him to wear it, though I know he set great store by it, for he kept it hanging in his room. But Jeth's young, like I said. He's not had no experience courting. That's why I thought it best to give him a little hint last Sunday after you'd gone. Just so it wouldn't come as a surprise."

"A hint? What hint?" Ginny spoke automatically. The idea that Jeth cared about her was too new. She remembered all the things he had done. Sympathized about her cousins. Kept the secret about Nona. Offered advice on subjects she had known nothing about. Given her the beautiful trinket box. And worked the distant fields alone while other men demanded that she stand admiringly by. Of course, he'd accepted pay for that, so it didn't count.

"Oh, I heard what Pastor Gilbert whispered to you last Sunday," explained Aunt Lizzie coyly. "Nothing wrong with my hearing yet. All about his joyful news. I reckoned he was about ready to pop the question. That's what I told Jeth. I didn't want him to be let down when he found out."

"Pastor Gilbert must have meant something else. He never asked me to marry him," Ginny told her quickly. "And even if he did, I'd turn him down."

"You would?" Aunt Lizzie did not bother to hide her astonishment. "He's a good catch, child. And you got to marry sometime. 'Course if you felt better waiting out the full year that's another matter. But there's not a soul would blame you if you didn't. Out here, where womenfolks is scarce, six months is understood."

"What did Jeth say when you told him about Pastor Gilbert?"

"Why as I recollect, he didn't say nothing." Aunt Lizzie's tear-stained face puckered in thoughtful lines. "He didn't have much to say at all that night. Went to bed early as I remember. Then the next morning he was

174

gone. There was just that letter." She broke off suddenly. "I declare. I'm that rattled, I forgot all about the other one."

"Other one?"

"Other letter. For you. Leastwise it's got your name on it, and since he'd went to all the trouble to put it in a envelope and stick it shut, I didn't feel right about peeking. You wait here. I'll get it." She trotted from the room and returned shortly with an envelope.

Ginny broke the seal and a gold piece tumbled into her hands. There was a sheet of paper, too.

"Dear Ginny"—Jeth had written—"I never meant to take pay for the work or vittles. I was joshing. I hope you and Pastor Gilbert will be real happy. Respectfully, Jethro Manning."

"What's he say?" Aunt Lizzie demanded eagerly, and after she had read the note, she asked sharply, "What's he mean about taking pay?"

"I said I'd pay him a dollar a day for his work. And he brought me meat from town when ours ran out. I paid him for that, too. He's given all the money back."

"Well, I should think so." Aunt Lizzie snorted indignantly. "I brung him up better than that. The meat was from my own meathouse, and my nephew don't take pay for helping out a friend." She shook her head with exasperation. "That's what I mean about Jeth being so young, thinking to josh you like that. Some things ain't to be joshed about. But the boy won't be eighteen till July."

"I don't think eighteen is so young," said Ginny. "It's three years older than me."

Aunt Lizzie put Ginny in Jeth's room that night. It was a small room, added to the cabin as an afterthought. There wasn't much in the way of furniture, just a bed and a chair. On pegs, driven into the unpeeled logs of the walls, hung some of Jeth's clothes. She recognized a blue shirt that she had often seen him wear. The high boots that stood in the corner were the same ones in which he had walked through the mud to check on her last spring. There was no sign of the striped necktie, and she wondered if he had taken it with him.

She felt a lump growing in her throat and after she had climbed into bed, she began to cry. Jeth Manning, you stupid, stupid boy, she thought. Why didn't you tell me? Why didn't you say something?

During the night Aunt Lizzie regained some of her composure. After breakfast, while Ginny did the dishes, she sat at the table and clasped her hands on the oilcloth surface.

"I been thinking," she began. "Likely that woman that stayed with you had white blood in her. Probably more than half. And for once, the white won over the savage. It don't happen often, but like they say, it's the exception that proves the rule."

Ginny shook her head. If Aunt Lizzie could only see Nona, she would realize such a thing was impossible. She turned to dispute the fact, but when she realized the older woman wasn't listening, she went back to scraping egg from the plates.

"And for all we know she could have been all white," Aunt Lizzie continued, warming to the idea. "Maybe she was stole from a wagon train when she was a baby and raised by the savages. Some of their heathen ways was bound to rub off, but inside she was as white as me and you."

This was too much. Ginny couldn't let Aunt Lizzie go on building up a fantasy in her mind. She had to face the truth.

"That couldn't be so, Aunt Lizzie," she said loudly. "Nona was all Indian."

"You can't be sure," insisted Aunt Lizzie stubbornly. "If she was born white, or even half-white, it would account for the way she acted—not stealing you blind or scalping you in your bed."

"Nona wouldn't think of such a thing," said Ginny indignantly. "She was good. And she did her share of the work every day without even being told."

"There, you see!" cried Aunt Lizzie triumphantly. "She couldn't have been all Injun because they don't act that way. Where'd you say she went?"

"Back to her own people, the Molallas."

"Poor thing," said Aunt Lizzie sympathetically. "Naturally she'd think of them that way, but somewhere there's a Christian family that's still mourning their lost child stolen away when she was too young to remember. It's sad to think on."

Ginny sighed helplessly. Aunt Lizzie was so good and kind, so quick to come to the aid of anyone who needed help. Why did she have to have this stubborn block about people of another race? No one would ever be able to change her mind either. Maybe her generation would always think that way. But Ginny resolved that her children, if she ever had any, would be different. She'd teach them to think more like Jeth, to realize that skin color had no bearing on what was inside a person.

"I hope you're not going to tell people that story you just made up," she said. "Because it is a story."

"No," decided Aunt Lizzie. "Way I see it, we best let things lie like they are now. We'll just say your cousin's gone, which she has, and that you're staying here a spell."

"But if people ask, if they find out about Nona, I think we should tell the truth," insisted Ginny. "I'm tired of lies."

"I don't hold with them neither," said Aunt Lizzie primly. "But what they don't know won't hurt them. So far nobody but us knows, and that's a blessing."

Ginny thought of Pastor Gilbert. He knew. But she was very sure that Pastor Gilbert would keep silent.

"And if it should leak out, well, I'll handle it then," Aunt Lizzie concluded grimly, getting to her feet. "Nobody around here's going to go against me, I can promise you that. Now we best get to the washing. Monday I was so rattled about Jeth leaving that it went plum out of my head. And yesterday I didn't feel like doing it neither. What folks'll say to see wash hanging out on a Wednesday, I don't know. But there it'll be."

Ginny helped with the washing, then volunteered to hang it out while Aunt Lizzie made the pie she had promised Josiah for dinner. She carried the heavy basket, heaped with wet clothes, out to the back yard where lines were strung between two poles.

As she lowered it to the ground, she was aware of a stirring in the barn. The click of metal. The whinny of a horse. No one should be in the barn this time of day!

She left her basket of laundry and advanced cautiously across the yard. There was the sound of the affectionate slap of a man's hand against a horse's rump, then a voice, muffled but familiar. "There you are, old girl. Eat up. You earned it."

"Jeth!" She ran the remaining steps and met him at the door. "Jeth! You're back!"

She had never been so glad to see anyone before in her life. She threw her arms around his neck and kissed him. Then his arms were around her and he was kissing her back.

"Why did you do it? Why did you run away like that? And leave a letter behind?" She pushed him away to look at him, his lopsided smile, his round blue eyes, the endearing cowlick in his hair. Maybe he wasn't the most handsome man in the world, but she wouldn't trade him for another. She didn't ever want him to go away again.

"It wasn't smart," he admitted ruefully. "All the way to Salem I kept thinking about everything Aunt Lizzie and Uncle Josiah had done for me. So I turned around. It wasn't right to go and leave just a letter the way I did."

"How about me? Was it right to leave me without saying a word?"

"I left you a letter. Didn't Aunt Lizzie give it to you? And I even wished you happiness with Pastor Gilbert."

"I'm not going to marry Pastor Gilbert," she told him quickly. "I'm going to marry you."

"Me?" It took him a minute to comprehend what she was saying, then a slow grin covered his face. It wasn't

179

lopsided this time. It spread straight across. "Are you proposing to me, Widow Mayhew?"

She knew she'd done an unmaidenly thing, throwing herself at a man that way. But then, she wasn't a maid. Not in the eyes of the law. She was a widow, and a widow should have special rights.

"Who else could I get to work my farm?" she asked.